A Wife

for

Ransom

WENDY MAY ANDREWS

Sparrow Ink
www.sparrowink.com

**They find themselves married,
but can they be a family?**

Ransom is just looking for a mother for his orphaned niece. The fact that she's from Boston is a bonus. Their arrangement allows him to get out of town.

Hannah needs a husband. Her new name will protect her siblings. The fact that he lives in the back of beyond gives them a place to hide. She hadn't counted on him being so appealing.

But what happens when they realize how very permanent their proxy marriage truly is?

Dedication

In this book Hannah will do whatever it takes to protect her family. Ransom marries her to protect his. Family is a strong theme I firmly believe in. I also believe that if the family you're born with isn't perfectly fabulous, you can make your own. This book is for my family and yours, both the one you got by chance and the one you made.

Acknowledgements

My beta readers are my writing lifeline – Marlene, Suzanne, Christina, Monique, and Alfred – you all helped Hannah and Ransom have a much better story. Thank you!

My editor, Julie Sherwood, is awesome. If you come across anything questionable in this book, it's my fault, not hers.

Special thanks to my parents for instilling a love of words and always supporting me in my endeavors.

And extra thanks to Mr. Andrews for ordering pizza when I'm on a deadline, for helping me figure out the best state to place my stories in, and for taking me to visit them when I need to visualize the story. You're the best!

Chapter One

"Ransom? What kind of a name is Ransom, anyway?"

Hannah rolled her eyes at her brother's question. The twelve-year-old boy was trying to be sophisticated and tough, but she knew he was struggling through his grief. Hannah wished she could let them stay in their familiar surroundings, at least until their grief was a little less fresh, but time was not a luxury they possessed at this time. She needed to get these arrangements finalized and get the children on the train before her uncle caught wind of her plans.

"I'd say it's a rather appropriate name under the circumstances," Sybil murmured, bringing a smile to Hannah's strained face.

Casting a wry glance at her friend before turning back to her brother, Hannah kept her tone calm and even. "It's a strong, old name. He was probably named after an ancestor. And, I will add, it is a name you will be careful never to make fun of."

Brent grunted in reply. Hannah should take exception to his lack of civility, but she took pity on him under the circumstances. "Could you please go get Maryanne? We'll be having tea shortly, and I'm sure she needs something to eat."

Her brother's expression as he left the room was a mutinous mixture. Hannah had to bite the inside of her cheek to keep her face serious. It was obvious her brother was torn between indignation that she would even consider him immature enough to stoop so low as to make fun of an unusual name. On the other hand, a part of him really wanted to indulge that immature side. Hannah wished her brother didn't have to grow up so suddenly. That was part of her motivation in making this decision. If she were married, her twelve-year-old brother wouldn't feel the need to try to be the man of the house.

Of course, she thought with a toughening mental stance, most of the reason she was marrying was so her uncle couldn't get his hands on the children. She begrudged her father's archaic thinking when he had his Will prepared. In his defense, she was sure he never expected the Will to be needed, at least not this part of it, anyway. Their parents had been young, spry, and healthy. There was no reason to expect Hannah would need to fight to keep her brother and sister with her, rather than allowing their uncle to take over guardianship of them.

But she would never allow that. She didn't trust Uncle Jason, and nothing anyone could say would convince her otherwise. She didn't like the way he had started looking at her when she had turned fifteen. For the last five years she had made every excuse she could think of to spend the least amount of time possible with him. It was only due to her mother's distraction with Hannah's much younger siblings that she had never noticed. But Hannah would have thought her father had enough sense not to leave any of them in their uncle's power.

She was well aware that her father didn't much care for his wife's brother. She had never confided in either of her parents about her discomfort around her uncle, but it was well known that the man coveted her father's fortune. Hannah's father had done everything in his power to help his brother-in-law be successful in his own right, but the man didn't want to actually work for his funds. He had already blown through the inheritance he had received when his own parents had died. Hannah wouldn't have expected her father to provide a situation in which he could get his hands on their inheritance as well. But he was the only family they had left. And to Hannah's father, there was nothing more important than family.

Hannah didn't disagree. There was nothing in this world more important to her than her brother and sister. It didn't matter how awkward the arrangements she was making were going to be for her. It would keep her brother and sister safe. So she would do it. And no one would ever know it was a trial for her, least of all her siblings. They must never realize or they would surely feel badly about it. No, they needed to remain children for as long as possible. That was Hannah's new goal in life.

She glanced out the window and thought how much her life had changed in the last few weeks. It was exactly three weeks ago today that she had been sitting in this very same room, talking with her mother, discussing which gowns they were going to have made. At that point, Hannah's main focus had been to have a good time as she continued her hunt for an appropriate husband. How her understanding of appropriate had changed in these past weeks. And her determination. When she had been discussing it with her mother, she had been half-hearted in her search. She had no intention of marrying this year. She would have rather enjoyed herself for at least one more year, preferably even two, but she hadn't wanted to let on to her mother, of course. Hannah's sweet mother wanted to see her firstborn settled and happy. How prophetic that had been. If her mother could see her now, she would be horrified.

But her mother wasn't there to see her now. Hannah tried her very best not to feel bitter about that. It surely wasn't her parents' fault they'd been killed. Hannah was just grateful the children hadn't been with them. She wasn't all alone in the world, even if she was alone in shouldering the burdens. But that wasn't to be thought of. The children were not burdens. It was merely the fight to keep them that was the burden. But after today, that fight would be over.

She would leave the arrangements in the trusted hands of the family lawyers. All she had to do was sign the papers Fred held and then present them to the lawyer in the morning, just before they climbed on the train. Uncle Jason wouldn't even know they were gone. And when he did find out, he wouldn't know where to start looking. It would give her a good head start. And there was little he would be able to do anyway. The lawyers had assured her it was legal and that they would keep her confidential matters confidential.

Staring off into the middle distance, she felt grateful to the government of Massachusetts for passing a law that allowed her to have separate economy. She had never really realized that single women had different rights than married ones. Not that either of them had all that many rights when compared with men, but at least now she would be able to retain ownership and control of her father's businesses until her brother was in a position to take over.

She wasn't going to raise an outcry over the fact that she wasn't going to be able to take over running the businesses herself. While she would like to think she was capable of doing so and doing it well, that was a footnote in her life right now. Her priority was her siblings. Keeping them safe was going to take all her energy for the next while. She had been assured that the businesses could look after themselves for a time. She wasn't so innocent as to think they would thrive without someone there to manage them firmly, but she was also experienced enough to understand that if it she were trying to firmly manage them herself they might flounder even worse. The law might say she had the right to own them, but many of the men who worked there would probably have disputed that fact.

Hannah shook her head with a sigh. That was neither here nor there. She turned her attention back to Sybil and Fred, who were being remarkably patient with her. Not that many moments had passed while she had been lost in her thoughts, but they were probably anxious to get on with their own affairs. She wasn't actually close friends with either of them, mere acquaintances, really. Hannah couldn't expect them to put their private affairs on hold while she sorted out her own. She appreciated the kindness and discretion on their part that had led them to seek her out and make the unusual suggestion. Hannah had heard the faintest rumor that they had been known to arrange convenient marriages, but she never would have thought she would find herself in need of their services. But when Sybil had visited a few days ago to express her sympathy and delicately inquire about Hannah's welfare, the subject had arisen and Hannah had found out all about marriage by proxy.

"You are certain he understands that I am bringing the children with me?"

"Yes, of course. Why would he mind you bringing them since part of your appeal for him is your willingness to take on the responsibility for his youngster as well?"

Hannah smiled. "Do you know, I haven't met all that many men who are so very egalitarian in their thinking?"

Sybil smiled gently while Fred chuckled. "I can see your point, Hannah, but yes, you needn't worry about that."

"And you didn't tell him everything about my brother's inheritance, right?"

"I said very little about that. But I promise you, he won't be coveting your brother's assets. He has sufficient of his own."

"Tell me again why he is willing to do this for us."

Fred's tone was one of strained patience, but he explained anyway. "As I told you before, he is anxious to set off for a project further west, but he cannot leave his child behind with no one to care for her. He needs a wife in case something happens to him. He entrusted me to find him someone trustworthy. When I heard about your situation, I knew you would be perfectly able to help each other out."

"So, he will not try to fight me for the assets?"

"He will not."

"But he'll be able to protect us from Uncle Jason?"

This time Fred hesitated slightly. Hannah noted it immediately.

"Why are you not so sure?"

"Well, it's just that, as I told you, he is anxious to be off further west."

"So he will not be present? Is that what you're saying?"

"That's right."

Hannah paused for a moment and then shrugged. "Well, that's probably just as well. I will have the legal protections that I require but won't be troubled with an actual husband to muddy up the waters as my siblings and I try to settle into a new life." She paused again. "Do you suppose he has hired help of any sort? Are there animals to be cared for or anything? Does he realize that I know so very little about the actual running of a household? I mean, I can run a household of staff, but the actual labor is something that I'm going to have to learn. Of course, if he isn't there to witness my struggles, I guess he shouldn't care all that much."

"I'm not fully certain of his situation with regards to hired help. But in your financial circumstances, you could probably hire help for yourself anyway, couldn't you?"

Hannah nodded. "We could, but we won't want to draw any attention to ourselves. Never mind. We'll figure it out when we get there. The main thing is we'll be safe from Uncle Jason, at least for a time. I just need the children to be a bit older before they are exposed to him. Don't get me wrong, I don't ever want them to be in his sphere of influence, but I will allow them to make their own decisions on the matter when they are older. He is the only family we have left besides each other. I cannot keep them from him indefinitely. But preferably until my brother is old enough to inherit. Then Uncle Jason won't want them in the same way. That's the only reason he wants them now. He or she who gets the children gets control of the inheritance. I, myself, couldn't care less about the money, but I will not let that man have the children."

"Very well, then, come and sign this paper, and you will be a married woman, thus fulfilling the stipulation in your father's Will that you be granted guardianship of your siblings if you are married."

"Such a stupid codicil," she grumbled as she approached and sat at the small table Fred was standing beside. She signed where he indicated, grateful that he had multiple copies for her to sign. It would be best if one were left with her lawyers just in case anything was disputed. It would have been even better if they could back date the document, but she wasn't going to risk it being nullified for something like that. She was absolutely certain Uncle Jason would fight her on this. She had to ensure there was nothing he could dispute. As it was, she had been able to prevent the lawyers from registering the final Will until after she had this finalized. She had to hope it would be enough. They seemed to think it was, but she was sure the law was wily and Uncle Jason would find a way. A woman wouldn't be able to stand against him. But since she would conveniently have a husband, she stood a better chance. She just hoped this Ransom fellow was as tough as his name implied.

She signed the final copy with a flourish, relieved that it was finished. Relieved, too, that she didn't feel any different as Fred grinned while offering her congratulations. "You are now a properly married woman. Congratulations, Mrs. Delaney."

Hannah blinked and then laughed. "You can stick with Hannah. Anything else will take some getting used to."

"Shall we celebrate?" Sybil inquired softly after she finished signing the few places that needed to be witnessed.

Hannah laughed again. "I think I'll celebrate by completing my packing. But the housekeeper will be bringing up tea shortly, and the children will be joining us. Please stay. Her scones are unbelievable. I plan to eat several, since it's doubtful I will have another as good for quite some time."

Sybil's smile was gentle. "Did you ask her for the recipe?"

"I did. I took your suggestion and asked for the recipe for all our favorite dishes. But even though I have spent a fair bit of time in the kitchens over the years, I think certain things are an inborn talent. Baking is not one that I was gifted. I will be able to make do. We will not starve. But there will be no scones."

"Do you truly think it's worth leaving?"

"Absolutely." Even Hannah could hear the conviction in her voice. She didn't have a single doubt about the decision she had made. Oh, of course, there were about a million doubts with regards to the sense it made to wed a stranger and pack the children up and move them across the country on such short notice. But she didn't have a single doubt about keeping them from their Uncle Jason. And the lawyers had assured her the only way she could do that was with a husband. So a husband she had gotten. Now she just had to meet him.

After tea and scones, Fred and Sybil left Hannah with her brother and sister to finish their preparations. As they took their leave, Sybil had extracted the promise from Hannah that she would let them know if she ran into any further difficulty. Hannah appreciated the sentiment, but there was nothing the kindly pair could do to help with her greatest struggle.

Hannah hoped her face did not reveal her concerns as she surveyed her siblings. They were both subdued. Hannah could see that Maryanne's eyes were still puffy from crying. Her heart clenched for the poor little girl. Ten years old was far too young to lose your parents. Twenty was too young, but at least she was an adult. She'd had her parents all to herself for eight years before her brother was born. And those eight years between them had allowed Hannah to have a much different relationship with their parents than her siblings had managed to yet develop. And now they never would. Hannah grieved for her own loss and for theirs. But she would have to deal with her emotions later. She now had to help them get ready for further change.

"Have you both selected your most favorite few things that must accompany us?"

Maryanne nodded sullenly while her brother glared at her. "I don't understand why you will only let us bring three things each."

"Brent, dear, you do realize we'll be travelling on the train for days, don't you? We will not have space for too much. We can send for more of our things later, but for now, we have to think of how much space we'll have."

Hannah didn't tell them that she didn't want to be noticed as they travelled. If they had too much baggage, it would be sure to draw attention. As it was, it would be hard to keep from being noticed. She might be an adult, but she was still young and looked it. She was planning to do as much as she could to look staid and severe, but she wasn't sure if she could add years to her face. From her experience, though, people didn't look beyond the obvious. They saw what they expected to see. So, she was going to present herself as her siblings' mother or nanny, as plain and uninteresting as she could manage.

Since they hadn't said anything more, Hannah gave a soft sigh and then prompted them, "I know you aren't happy about this, but it's what we need to do. Please, make sure you're ready early in the morning. I will be visiting the lawyer first thing, and then I'll stop here briefly to collect you before heading to the train station.

It is imperative that we be ready on time. I swear to you, I wouldn't make you do this if it wasn't important."

Their response was muted, but they both nodded. Maryanne even approached and gave her a quick hug. "Doesn't mean we have to like it, though."

Through a mist of tears in her eyes, Hannah smiled. "No, you don't have to like it. I don't like it either, but we're going to try to make the best of it. You'll see. Riding the train will be an adventure."

Chapter Two

Nerves jangled in Hannah's stomach. *Maybe if I don't tell the lawyers, it won't actually be true. Maybe I didn't actually just marry a stranger in the front parlor of my house by proxy.* She felt a well of hysterical laughter rising and fought to quell it. Like that philosophical question she had heard discussed at one of her parents' art evenings: If a tree falls in the woods with no one around, does it make a sound? Well, she had the signed paper in her reticule to prove that even if she didn't tell anyone, she had married one Mr. Ransom Delaney. Which made her Mrs. Hannah Delaney. Again, she had to fight the hysteria threatening her. But, she reminded herself, Mrs. Hannah Delaney is a brand-new person and can decide exactly who she's going to be. *And I have decided she will be fierce. No hysteria allowed.*

Hannah lifted her chin and stared straight in front of her, refusing to be cowed even by her own tumultuous thoughts. She rose to her feet as soon as the clerk entered the room.

"Mr. Mulroney will see you now."

"Thank you, Charles." Hannah ignored the shy, hopeful smile the clerk cast her way. Handsome, young, local men were of no use to her. And she didn't need one anymore, anyway, she reminded herself as she stepped into the handsomely appointed office of her family's lawyer.

The room was large. The wood paneling gave it warmth although the very large, imposing desk at one end would have been intimidating if she hadn't been familiar with the type. Her father had one almost exactly like it in his library at home. Hannah had grown up surrounded by powerful men. This lawyer did not make her nervous. Only the nature of her errand did. But Hannah Delaney was not the nervous sort, she reminded herself.

"Thank you for seeing me so early, Mr. Mulroney."

"I take it you have met the requirements of your father's Will."

"Yes. I have a copy for your records." She handed over one copy of her signed marriage license. "I trust this will be held in the strictest confidence."

The lawyer looked affronted momentarily, but then he smiled warmly. "You can be absolutely certain that your news will not reach the ears of your Uncle Jason through anyone from this office, at least not until the official reading of the Will."

"Thank you. I assure you, I do not mean to cast doubt on anyone's trustworthiness. But you know how concerned I am on the subject."

"I do, my dear, and no offense was taken. How else may we be of service?"

"I think everything has already been discussed sufficiently. I will contact you once I have made arrangements through which we can communicate. I will appreciate monthly reports once we have set up a means of remaining in contact. I've already made arrangements for my household staff to find work elsewhere, except for a very small crew. For now, we aren't completely closing up the house, but that will probably have to be done eventually."

"It does seem that you've thought of everything."

Hannah was torn between delight over the approval she saw in the older man's eyes and disappointment that the man seemed so surprised. *Did he not realize that even young women can have a few thoughts in their heads?* She could feel that her smile was on the cool side, but she kept it in place anyway through force of will.

"Are you very certain you've made the right choice, Miss Bowman? I cannot think this is what your father had in mind when he made that provision in his Will."

"My father thought he was invincible, so he didn't really think about his Will all that much. I rather think it was you or one of your colleagues who had that stipulation made, and I'm very sure this isn't what my father expected."

The lawyer looked as though he were going to protest, but Hannah didn't bother allowing it. She didn't hold a grudge. There was no time and it wasn't worth the energy.

"But it's there and needs to be lived with. I will not allow my uncle to have guardianship of Maryanne or Brent. So, I need a husband. No one we know here in

Boston will do. From what I've learned of this Mr. Delaney, he will do nicely. I am no longer the romantic debutante I was a few weeks ago. I will do whatever it takes to protect my brother and sister."

"That's an admirable attitude, Miss Bowman."

"It's Mrs. Delaney, now," she reminded him softly as she got to her feet and held her hand out to shake his. The older man blinked as though he didn't recognize her. That was quite all right. Hannah barely recognized herself. She smiled as he shook her hand firmly. The old codger had decided to respect her. There was nothing more Hannah could ask for.

Her stomach clenched again as she left his office and headed for home. It was time to collect the children and depart for their new lives. She just hoped the staff had managed to get their things loaded discretely and everyone was ready to go when she got there.

Her trust had been well placed. The housekeeper was waiting for her in the foyer when Hannah stepped through the front door.

"Everything is as you requested, Miss Hannah," the older woman said while she dabbed at her red eyes with a handkerchief. "Are you absolutely certain I cannot come with you?"

"I am certain, Marilla, at least for now. We mustn't draw any attention to ourselves while we travel West. You understand why, don't you?"

"Oh, I do, Miss, but I just cannot bear to think of the three of you going off all alone like this. Your parents would have my head if they knew of it."

Hannah could feel her face pulling into a grim expression as she tried to answer the older woman. "Well, they should've made better arrangements if they were so set against something like this." At the housekeeper's aghast expression, Hannah offered a conciliatory smile. "Never mind about that. I've made all the necessary arrangements. There's nothing to go wrong. Brent, Maryanne, and I will be perfectly safe. We will stick to our room as much as possible. And with the speed of train travel now, we'll be to our destination before we've even had time to get settled. Then we'll be perfectly safe once my husband is there to take care of us."

Hannah wanted to roll her eyes, but she knew that was what the sweet older woman wanted to hear. And she was right. Marilla brightened up immediately.

"Yes, of course, your husband will know just what to do." But then the woman finally realized what she was saying. "Of course, I cannot be perfectly settled about you going off with a man none of us have ever met or even heard of before. Are you absolutely certain about this, Miss? You really ought to take one of us with you, just to be completely certain."

"Marilla, I promise you, I have thought it all through and am absolutely certain. I have discussed the matter thoroughly with Mr. Mulroney and his associates."

"Well, yes, they are wise men to guide you, of course." The housekeeper dabbed at her eyes some more, and Hannah softened toward her as usual.

Pulling the older woman into her arms for a brief hug, Hannah assured her, "I promise you, I will write as soon as we arrive so that you know we are safe and sound. Will that help to reassure you?" There was a vigorous nod so Hannah continued. "And you will be remaining here to look after everything for us so it will be fit for our return."

"Oh, yes, of course, Miss, you can count on me to be sure. Everything will be kept spic and span, even if you aren't here."

"I knew we could count on you, Marilla." She briskly changed the subject. "Do you know if the children are ready? I just have to change my clothes."

"Oh, but you look so nice already, Miss."

Hannah ignored the words. There was no way she could wear the handsome velvet suit she had on and expect anyone to think she was a humble mother of two youngsters. When she didn't respond, the housekeeper remembered her question.

"Yes, Master Brent and Miss Maryanne are in the dining room just finishing their breakfast, but all the luggage is loaded as you requested and they're dressed and ready whenever you are."

"Thank you so much, Marilla. I will be with them in just a couple minutes." She didn't wait for a reply and dashed up the stairs. It wasn't polite debutante behavior, but she was no longer a debutante, she reminded herself with the first real grin she had felt in the weeks since her parents' sudden death.

~~~

As Hannah quickly changed from her fashionable clothes for visiting the lawyer into something she deemed more appropriate for the matronly guardian of two youngsters, she couldn't keep the memories at bay.
~~~

It had been a bright, sunny day. There had been no environmental foreshadowing of the terrible news they were about to receive. In hindsight, it seemed dreadfully unfair that something so earth shattering should take place on a sunny day. Hannah shoved away the ridiculous thought. Even if it had been raining torrentially, there was no good time to find out their loving, wonderful parents had been killed.

Hannah shuddered to think of it. The industrial accident that had destroyed half the factory was still being investigated, but Hannah wondered for what felt like the millionth time whether or not it was wise to take the children by train. But trying to travel by a horse-drawn conveyance all the way to Nebraska would take weeks, maybe even months, while the train would only take them seven days. But the threat of an explosion made her throat clench. She just hoped they had been successful in their bid to have their room as far away from the engine as possible.

Of course, with taking a twelve-year-old boy onto a train, the engine would be impossible to avoid entirely, but Hannah would hope and pray for their safety. She had to choose the lesser of two evils. From what she had heard and read, train travel was remarkably safe these days. And it would get the three of them away and safe from Uncle Jason. *On the other hand, no doubt Father had thought that factory was safe to visit as well.*

Hannah pushed the tumultuous thoughts from her head. They were not in the least helpful. The train tickets were purchased, their bags were packed, and she had to get downstairs to make sure the children got on that train. She could not allow them to remain in

Boston with the potential of being at the mercy of their uncle. *The risk of the train is minimal. Deep breaths, deep breaths.* Hannah regarded her pale reflection and grimaced. She looked dreadful. But that would be to their advantage. She didn't look like a wealthy young woman from a big city, and that was all she needed.

She had forced herself to do as she had admonished the children. Her baggage was as light as she had been able to reasonably make it. With only her most favorite book and all the important papers along with personal garments, she had never packed so lightly even for a few days away, let alone packing up her entire life. But it was necessary for the circumstances. That was becoming her personal mantra. Whatever was necessary for the circumstances. She was well aware that the expression on her face was grim. She tried to plaster on a smile for the sake of the servants and the children as she left her room and returned to the foyer.

"Oh, Miss Hannah, what have you done to yourself?"

Hannah's lips stretched into a spontaneous smile. It couldn't be helped. She was glad her effort had paid off.

"Where ever did you find such a dreadful outfit?"

"It's far from dreadful," Hannah soothed.

"Well, it's far from acceptable attire for Miss Bowman," Marilla retorted.

"Perhaps so, but I'm no longer Miss Bowman. I do not wish to draw attention, and I don't want to look like a debutante from Boston." There was a mirror in the foyer and Hannah gazed critically at her reflection. "I was hoping to be able to pass as the children's mother, but I don't think I quite managed it."

The housekeeper fluttered her handkerchief as she dabbed at her eyes. "Your mother would have fits if she saw you."

"Fits of laughter, I would say," Brent interrupted, relieving Hannah of the need to soothe the housekeeper. "You look strange, Han."

"Too strange, do you suppose? I don't want to draw attention to myself, that's the entire point."

"Then I think you were successful. No one will want to look at you for long."

"Very good, then let us be off." Hannah ignored her brother's churlishness. She didn't think he was exaggerating. And she didn't want anyone looking at her. It was perfect. She herded the children into the carriage and they were off.

Chapter Three

When they pulled to a stop in front of the train station, Hannah was pleased to see that her brother was finally pulling himself out of his sullen mood. No twelve-year-old boy could stay moody when confronted with the prospect of riding in a train. It was to be a first for both of the youngsters. Hannah, herself, had only been in a train once before. She felt another lurch of nerves but chose to ignore it. She had been assured countless times that train travel was perfectly safe. She needn't think about the speed at which they'd be travelling, nor of the powerful engine that would be pulling them. And if she needed to think of it, she should rejoice that the speed would be removing them so swiftly from the presence of her dreadful Uncle Jason.

With a determined smile, Hannah took the hands of her brother and sister and stepped down from the carriage. She needed to keep a firm hand on the youngsters. In their excitement, she couldn't trust them not to wander off. It would be the worst possible development if she were to lose them just as they were about to depart.

Hannah was grateful for the porters who were bustling around, transporting their baggage to the correct train car. She was relieved, too, that she had been able to convince the staff to remain at home. It would not have supported her story of being an average housewife if she had servants hanging off her on the platform. And watching the housekeeper sob into her handkerchief wasn't the last view she wanted to carry away with her of Boston, either.

Within moments, they were in the train getting settled into their small room, and the train started to chug away from the station. They had cut it too close, Hannah thought with another sickening lurch of her stomach. But they had made it. The children were safe. They were on their way. Heading to the unknown. But it was an unknown she could control. She had the resources to be able to control it. Yes, she had married a stranger based on a trusted acquaintance's recommendation. That was doubtless a crazy thing to do. But it was the only way to achieve her ends. And it gave her the means to be able to provide for the children and keep them safe.

Hannah's head was starting to ache as the thoughts chased themselves around in her head. A month ago she would never have been able to picture herself in this situation. It was amazing what you could manage to do when it was necessary.

She tried to join in Brent's enthusiasm for the train and managed to listen with at least a semblance of a smile as he described in detail what was happening in the engine compartment.

"How do you know so much about this?" she marveled.

"Father took me with him a couple months ago when he was viewing the place where the engines are made. I think they were trying to impress him, so they told me everything." Brent chuckled as he remembered the occasion. "I don't think Father cared too much, but I loved it."

The laugh died suddenly in his throat as he remembered that he would have no further experiences like that with their father. Hannah watched helplessly as the boy's face crumpled. She then watched in amazement, as he seemed to collect himself and stem the tide of his grief. It was as though the boy refused to succumb to his sadness in that moment.

"Do you think they would let me see the engine while it's working?" he asked as his enthusiasm began to return.

Hannah swallowed her temptation to object. "You'll have to ask one of the porters. Perhaps after we've been travelling for a day or two, once they've gotten to know you, they'll be more willing to recommend you to the engineer."

Brent's eyes lit up. "That's a brilliant idea."

Hannah was glad she hadn't denied him directly. She wasn't sure if they would allow it, but she wasn't going to pay for the experience, as their father would have done. Hannah needed them to blend in. So Brent was just a boy eager to see the engine. If the engineers allowed it, Hannah would swallow her fears on her brother's behalf and allow it. It was the first time he had laughed since their parents' death. She wasn't about to discourage his delight in anything.

Turning her attention to Maryanne, Hannah's heart sank as she saw the little girl staring listlessly out the window.

"Is it a nice view, pumpkin?"

"Don't call me that. That's what Father called me," she objected without turning to face her sister.

"Everyone called you that," Hannah pointed out before conceding. "But if you don't want me to call you that, I won't. I'm sorry. It just slipped out from habit."

Maryanne hunched her shoulder and Hannah bit her lip. "Do you two want to get settled in here for a little bit or should we go exploring?"

"I want to stay here."

"Let's go exploring."

They spoke simultaneously and Hannah could have smacked herself in the forehead. This outcome should have been foreseeable. Of course, Brent would want to go exploring. And it was no surprise that the listless little girl wouldn't want to go anywhere. Hannah bit her lip, debating what was best. Brent was twelve years old. She should be able to allow him out of her sight. She was well aware that he had been wandering their neighborhood before their parents' death. But that was before he was in danger from their Uncle Jason. Since she was almost certain they had gotten away without his knowledge, she should be able to allow Brent to go exploring on his own.

"Swear to me you will not exit this train without my knowledge."

"Hannah," he began, whining.

"Promise me or you won't leave this room without me."

He huffed impatiently. "Fine, I promise."

"Good. And swear to me you'll be careful."

"You're worse than Mother," he complained.

"That doesn't sound like much of a promise," Hannah replied, ignoring the pang of guilt that assailed her for a moment.

Brent huffed again. "I swear, Hannah, I will be as careful as if there was a nursemaid following me around. And I won't leave the train without you."

"Even if the train stops?"

"Even if the train stops. Now can I go?"

"Very well. But you ought to come back in about an hour, as we'll probably be starting to get hungry and will need to find some luncheon."

Brent didn't bother replying, just ran out of the room without a backward glance, allowing the door to bang behind him. Hannah turned her attention to her sister, stifling her sigh.

Sitting down next to her, Hannah put her arm around the young girl. "Are you going to stare out the window much longer or would you like to help me tidy up our things?"

"I think I'll look a little longer," she answered before turning to Hannah with a small smile. "It actually is interesting, Han, I'm not just being sad."

Hannah returned her sister's smile. "I'll take your word for it, Mare. It just looks like fields to me."

"But how often have we really seen fields?" the little girl pointed out with a reasonable air.

Hannah's smile turned into a grin. "I guess you've got me there. Very well, you watch the scenery and keep me apprised if it changes much while I try to make a little bit of order here. Then, we should go look around a little bit, too, so we know where things are."

"All right, Hannah. Thank you for not minding me sitting for a bit. I just need to collect myself."

Hannah bit her lip over her sister's words, torn between amusement and dismay. It was funny that the little girl would word it that way, but Hannah didn't want Maryanne feeling the need to collect herself. The child should be eager to explore and shouldn't have cares to sort out. But there was nothing Hannah could do about it at the moment. She needed to do some self-collecting of her own.

After tidying up their bags and making sure the beds were made and ready for them later, Hannah was finally able to nudge Maryanne into movement. She couldn't believe how fascinated her sister was with the passing scenery. Hannah asked her about it when they finally left the room.

Maryanne shrugged. "I've never seen so much space, Hannah. Don't you realize that even though we have a bigger yard than most, no one in Boston actually has much space? Even when we go to the park, it's not like here. All these fields. I can't decide if I love it or hate it."

Hannah laughed. "I didn't realize you were being so introspective while we travelled. Let me know what you decide. I hope you will decide you don't hate it because

I'm rather certain there will be plenty of space at our destination."

Maryanne didn't actually grin back, but she looked a little less troubled than she had been for the past few weeks, much to Hannah's relief. And she finally appeared somewhat interested in their current surroundings as they walked down the hallway of the swaying train car. Hannah's stomach wasn't sure about the swaying, but she chose to ignore the churning, grateful that neither of the children appeared troubled by the motion. Not that they had yet found Brent, but when she had last seen him he had been the picture of health.

"Do you think we'll find Brent?" she asked in attempt to make conversation with her sister.

"Only if we're going to see the engines, I would imagine," was Maryanne's reply.

"Oh dear. I should have made him promise he wouldn't go there without me."

"It's probably better if he went alone, don't you think?"

"Why is that?" Hanna was horrified by her sister's observation.

"He won't be viewed as a child if he's on his own. I think the men would be more interested in talking to him if you aren't there. If you're there, they'll be too busy making eyes at you to pay him any mind."

Hannah felt heat climb into her cheeks. She tried to deny her sister's words, but Maryanne's gaze turned withering as only a sibling's could.

"I'm now a married woman." Hannah's declaration only served to make the girl giggle.

"That doesn't change how you look, Han."

Hannah glanced down at her hands and realized she should be wearing a ring to indicate her married state. She didn't think her sister was completely accurate in her thoughts about men's attentions, but it was true that Hannah often attracted unwanted attention. She prompted her sister to return momentarily to their room where she scrambled in search of her parents' rings. She didn't have anything else that would serve the purpose. She felt some qualms about putting on her mother's wedding ring but decided it was for the greater good. She ignored all other adornments, reminding her sister that they were hoping to draw little attention to themselves.

Maryanne's smile was mischievous. "I don't think that will work too well."

"Why not?" Hannah demanded.

"For one thing, I don't think Brent will be able to help himself. For the other, you're too pretty. Wearing ugly clothes and a wedding ring doesn't change that."

Hannah shushed her sister. "We have to at least try."

"You never did explain why we're so desperate to avoid Uncle Jason."

Hannah blinked at Maryanne's observation. "I didn't?" Hannah realized that was probably true. Not that she really wanted to tell the children. She wished they could remain as innocent as possible for as long as possible. But it would be for their protection if she told them.

"We will discuss it when we all return to our room after we eat," she promised. "Shall we see if this train has a library?"

"Oh, yes, please," Maryanne was easily distracted by the thought of books.

Hannah wanted to take advantage of the luxury while they had the opportunity. If she had understood correctly, the train accommodations would become decidedly more primitive the further west they travelled. She was grateful that this first leg of the journey would be close to what they were all used to. There was time enough for them to become familiar with deprivation later when they changed trains.

Maryanne was delighted with the small library car. There were still a couple of windows where she could keep her eye on the passing scenery while also perusing the surprisingly good selection of books. Hannah couldn't help the deep, appreciative breaths she was taking. The room, with its dark wood paneling wherever there weren't shelves, reminded her of their father's library at home. It even smelled the same, like wood smoke and old books. Hannah felt a frisson of déjà vu slither down her spine. Like if she turned her head fast enough she would be able to catch a glimpse of her father leaning over his desk or hiding behind his newspaper. While her mind knew their parents were gone, it was taking a while for her heart to accept that knowledge. She stopped sniffing, hoping her sister didn't notice the similarities.

After about fifteen minutes, maybe it was less, but it felt like three hours to Hannah, she finally couldn't bear the room anymore and she prompted her sister to leave.

"Let's walk all around first and figure out where everything is and see if we can find Brent. We can come back here and pick out some books to take to our room later."

With reluctance, Maryanne agreed with one condition. "Could I take this book now? If I don't, someone else will come along and take it for themselves."

When Hannah glanced at the cover, she doubted her sister needed to be concerned that others would want to take it from her, but she would never want to discourage either of her siblings from learning or reading so she kept her face neutral and agreed. She thought it unlikely anyone else would be as fascinated with flora and fauna as her sister seemed to be suddenly. The large book appeared to be a scientific textbook. It was not at all what Hannah had expected the child to select.

"Let's take it back to our room now, though. It's too big to be carrying around with us."

Maryanne happily agreed and Hannah was relieved. If the girl already had a book, maybe she could avoid the library for a day or two.

Within a few minutes, they were back to exploring. Not that there was all that much for them to see. Several cars were just a long corridor with doors on either side, exactly like the one they were staying in. They were not allowed into the luggage car, where things were being transported, which made sense to Hannah and was a relief. If they weren't allowed in there, neither were others, so their things ought to be safe. She hadn't told Maryanne and Brent, but there were a few more things travelling with them to their final destination. Hannah had realized they would need additional, warmer clothes as well as fabrics in order to be able to make whatever they didn't yet realize they needed. And while there were probably towns nearby she could travel to in order to purchase what they would need, she wanted to feel supplied, at least to a certain extent. She had tried to keep the volume of their luggage to a reasonable level, but she had to find the balance between having enough and not too much to draw an excessive amount of attention to their little traveling family.

She and Maryanne passed through a car of seated passengers, which prompted some questions from the little girl.

"Why are they just sitting there?"

"I think it's likely they didn't want to pay for a room. When Wilbur was buying our tickets, he said there were different prices, one of the prices was for just a seat."

"You mean they don't have somewhere to sleep?"

"Well, you could see that some of them were sleeping in their seat."

"But that will hurt their necks, won't it?"

"Eventually, yes. Maybe they aren't going so very far."

Maryanne's face was dubious. "It makes our room seem much more luxurious, doesn't it?"

Hannah grinned. "Very much so."

They kept walking and finally arrived in the dining car. Suddenly, both girls' stomachs began to growl in response to the variety of smells wafting from the kitchen.

"I do hope we find Brent soon. I'm starving."

Hannah smiled over her sister's exclamation. Her smile widened as they saw the very boy they were looking for enter the room from the opposite direction.

"What perfect timing," Hannah commented. "We were just wondering if we would need to send a search party."

A look of guilt travelled swiftly across Brent's face. "Did I lose track of the time? I'm sorry, I truly meant to keep my promise. I was on my way back to our room, I swear."

"Don't trouble yourself. We've been exploring, too. We just both realized how hungry we are when we arrived here. So, it's perfect timing." Hannah realized she was repeating herself, but she was determined to keep a façade of good spirits for the children's sake, especially while they both seemed to be less melancholy than they had been.

A waiter was trying to beckon them to a table, so Hannah quickly shepherded her siblings in his direction. Within moments they had placed their orders and were left on their own with glasses of juice in front of the children and a warm cup of tea for Hannah, which she sincerely hoped would settle her nervous stomach.

"Now tell us, did you see everything you wanted to see?"

Brent launched into an enthusiastic description of all that he had seen and done in the hour or so they had been apart. It was the most animated Hannah had seen him since their parents had died. For that alone, she realized she had made the right decision leaving when they had. A change of scenery would do them all good.

Of course, she still doubted that completely changing their lives so drastically was for their very best when it came to their mental well-being. She had actually discussed the matter with their family physician, as she had been concerned that she might do them harm by making them face such a significant life change when their entire lives had already been thrown into disarray by their parents' sudden death. He had assured her that children were resilient and would be able to manage just fine. She hoped he was right. It wouldn't speed up their mourning period, she was sure. But maybe the fresh start would be better than the constant reminders that their parents were never coming back when they kept expecting to bump into them whenever they turned a corner.

Hannah stifled her sigh. She had so many things to concern herself. She thought with a momentary pang how uncomplicated her life had been a month ago. The only concern she had then was which seamstress to frequent and which gown to purchase for the next ball she was to attend. It was a simple, if shallow, life. Now she was solely responsible for Brent and Maryanne and needed to manage all three of their well-being.

Besides whatever added responsibilities her new husband would expect her to take on, she reminded herself with a bit of a start. She had been preoccupied with her concerns about keeping the children safe, but now that they were well on their way, her mind started to assail her with concerns about all that she still did not know.

35

Chapter Four

As Maryanne took over questioning Brent about what he'd learned about the train, Hannah allowed her mind to drift to the letter of introduction Fred had given her from her new husband. Apparently, the man had realized he would be wedding a stranger and had the foresight to tell her a little bit about himself. She had read the message so many times she had it memorized.

My dear good woman,

I address you this way since I trust that Fred will have chosen wisely for me, so I know he is sending me a kind, gentle woman to partner with.

Hannah had to smile over that. It was nice that he had such confidence in Fred. But she rather thought he was going to be sadly mistaken. She didn't think she was gentle. Maybe kind, if her mood was right. She sighed. She would have to try to be both kind and gentle, if that was what he was expecting. Her mother had been a kind, gentle, loving woman. She would try to imitate her. That would make it easier. Whenever she faced a situation, she would just have to figure out what her mother would do in the given situation. She continued pondering the letter.

My name is Ransom Delaney. I have lived in Nebraska for the past eight years. I have known Fred since we were boys. We were classmates at school. We went together to university, but I couldn't bear the classroom for the full four years required to complete it. After two, I left to find my own way in life out West. Fred and I have remained loosely in touch through letters and my sporadic trips home to visit my brother.

I now find myself in possession of my young niece. Her parents died when the flu swept through Boston last year. This is why I am in such desperate need of a wife. And I thought one from Boston would be best, since you would understand where the girl is coming from and should be able to help her grow up, as my brother and sister-in-law would have wished.

Since you are willing to accept an arrangement such as this, I'm assuming you face desperate circumstances of your own. I am willing and eager to help you with those as soon as you arrive here. I am healthy, of reasonable intelligence, and of above average means. We will manage to sort out your situation, I am sure.

I have a large house with plenty of land, so if you have children, there will be space for them to grow up. There is also a school nearby. It might not be quite the standard you would be able to find in Boston, but I am sufficiently satisfied with it to send my niece there.

If you have need of financial assistance to finalize your arrangements to travel to me, be sure to apply to Fred for the needed funds, and I will ensure he is reimbursed. Godspeed in your travels. I look forward to meeting you.

Yours sincerely,

Ransom Delaney

On the surface, the letter had told her very little. But when she made an effort to read between the lines, it had filled her with confidence that Fred had found her the perfect solution. The man had no idea or expectation of her funds; he was offering to pay for her expenses. That was a relief. He must not be completely broke. Not that she would begrudge him some of her finances. It was the least she could do for him, considering what he was doing for her and her family. But since it was not his motivation, it made him more appealing to her.

There were also no spelling or grammar errors in his letter. He mentioned that he didn't complete his education, but he *was* educated; she appreciated that. Not that she was so highly educated herself. Even though the university was now willing to accept female applicants, her father hadn't been willing to allow her to apply. That had been a huge disappointment to Hannah, but at least she was well read and her father had allowed her to attend some of the lectures that the university opened to the public. If her new husband were educated, he would be able to help Brent prepare for further education, as well. Surely, with the responsibilities Brent would have to take on when he was a bit older, he would need as much education as Hannah could arrange for him.

Then, too, there was the fact that he was open to her having children. Not that she did, really. She had the responsibility for her siblings. And they would always be a part of her life. So, it was the final reason she had accepted Fred's offer of marrying her by proxy to this Mr. Delaney. If he were willing to accept her siblings, she would happily accept his niece.

It was still certainly strange that she had not yet met the man she was married to. She listened absently to Brent and Maryanne chattering away about the scenery, allowing her gaze to remain unfixed out the window, hoping the children would think she was following their conversation, when in reality she was trying to imagine what her new husband was going to be like. She had surmised from his letter that he was kind and intelligent. And the fact that he was childhood friends with Fred told her he must be of an age with Fred. Hannah hadn't asked, but she would guess late twenties considering he had been out West for eight years after leaving university after two years. Since she, herself, was not yet twenty-one, it was a little old for her on one hand, but she would be grateful for his experience since she had so very little.

That was now her one of her biggest concerns. She knew how to run a household staffed with employed people. But she would have to learn to do things for herself. She strongly doubted there were many housemaids for hire in the West. And if she asked for a butler, she'd probably be laughed out of town. At least she was confident in her ability to keep them well-fed. She had been allowed to spend time in the kitchens since she was a small child and had managed to pick up many of her family's cook's tips and tricks. And, too, once she knew what she was about to do, she had spent an entire day in the kitchen picking the staff's minds to make sure she knew as much as she possibly could.

But that was the extent of her knowledge. She was reasonably sure she would be able to keep a house clean. Surely that wouldn't be difficult. Doing the laundry might be an issue, though. Marilla, the housekeeper, had tried to explain everything to her, but it had all run together in a blur. Hannah had asked Marilla to write it all down for her, but she hadn't even had a minute to review the notes, so she wasn't sure if they would do her any good or not. Perhaps Mr. Delaney knew how to do laundry.

And then there were the animals. Fred had explained that Mr. Delaney would most likely have a farm. So, she might be expected to milk cows or goats. And she would also probably be expected to assist in growing things like vegetables. Of course, she could get the children to help, but it all sounded like a great deal of work. She would like to think she was capable of working hard, but she had never really been tested in that regard before. The closest she had ever come to working was when she had been organizing the charity ball last spring. And she had so much help for that. And it was really merely a matter of making lists and delegating. She rather suspected there wouldn't be anyone she could delegate many of her tasks to once the children were in school. But at least, if they were in school, there would be no audience to witness her triumphs or failures. Except her new husband.

That was the challenge. She would be expected to spend time with the man. There would probably be intimacies expected. With a stranger. Hannah's queasy stomach, which had settled nicely with the tea, returned with a vengeance, and she had to breathe steadily through her nose to prevent herself from becoming sick. It was clearly time for a change of subject.

"Has anyone checked which will be our first stop and how long that stop might be?"

Both of the children blinked at her, surprised by her sudden turn of the subject.

"You weren't paying at all attention, were you?" Brent accused. "We were talking about that ten minutes ago."

"You were?" Hannah was horrified. She thought she had kept at least half her ear trained on their conversation. She felt heat flooding her face, and she was contrite. "I'm truly sorry, Brent. I've already had a long day and I think the tiredness is getting to my brain."

Her brother didn't look fully convinced but he was somewhat mollified. Luckily, at that moment, their meal finally arrived and the moment passed as everyone tucked into the surprisingly delicious smelling food.

Hannah wouldn't have thought she would be able to stomach anything given the circular motion of her thoughts and the upheaval in her midsection, but since she had ordered a rather bland meal, she was able to eat most of it. She hadn't been lying to her brother. She had already lived through a very long day. She had been up before the sunrise, overseeing the final packing, before she had returned to the lawyer's office to present them with her signed marriage certificate. Now with her stomach filling, she would happily sleep for a week. Of course, with her new responsibilities toward the children, she wouldn't be able to sleep so long, but she would claim as much sleep as she possibly could.

Thankfully the rest of the meal passed without incident. By the time everyone was fed, Brent was no longer holding a grudge toward his sister and peace reigned as they settled into their room for the night.

They settled into a routine over the next week. Their stops in different cities weren't exceptionally long, but Hannah did allow the children to get off and explore as long as they remained within her sight. Hannah hadn't cared much for the appearance of some of the locations, fearing for their safety. She was grateful for her foresight in wearing older, less fashionable clothing. Passing the three of them off as a mother with her two children caused them to attract far less attention, and they managed to make it all the way to their destination without being robbed or accosted. A fact for which she would be eternally grateful. No one ever really *asked* if she was the children's mother, but in her mind, that's what Hannah was portraying. Either way, they travelled undisturbed, a fact for which she was eternally grateful.

Hannah hadn't realized that she had been quite so protected all her life but on the third day of their trip she realized suddenly that this was the first time she had ventured from her home without a maid or steward in tow. That she was the one needing to offer protection rather than receive it was a disconcerting thought for her. She was grateful that she hadn't been called upon to provide any actual protection to the children other than with her presence. While her father had insisted that she be taught a few tricks for her own preservation when she had turned fourteen, Hannah wasn't certain if she would remember any of them if she were actually faced with a situation warranting them.

Finally, the last day of their journey dawned brightly. As the three occupants of their small train car began to stir, there was a definite air of excitement combined with trepidation, despite the silence. Or so it seemed to Hannah, anyway, but she might have been projecting her own thoughts onto the children, she realized as her eyes refused to remain closed. They had changed trains at one point on the fifth day, onto a different train company, heading a little bit more in a northerly direction. And they would arrive at their last stop mid-afternoon, if the steward were accurate in his prediction.

They had been fortunate on this journey. There had been no difficulties of a technical nature. The tracks held up under them, the engines chugged along; there were no breakdowns, or inordinate delays. Hannah's days of limbo were just about over. Her stomach clenched. She would indeed be someone's wife as soon as she stepped off the train this afternoon. She would be Hannah Delaney. Well, maybe Hannah Bowman Delaney. She had no intention of separating herself from Brent and Maryanne. While she had to acknowledge her husband's contribution to their safety, and his position in her life, by taking his name, she wasn't going to leave off her history. Surely, he would understand that. He was from Boston after all. It wasn't uncommon for a wife to just tack her husband's name on at the end instead of replacing her previous last name completely. With a brisk nod, she felt more settled in her heart. She wasn't ready to give up her family, even if she had committed herself to another one. She would just have to accommodate both.

Since they hadn't fully unpacked, there was little to do to get ready for the end of their journey. After Hannah had overseen both children's dress and grooming, they were ready for the day. Hannah couldn't bear their restlessness so she allowed them to venture out on their own.

"Do not allow Maryanne out of your sight, Brent. Promise me."

With a long-suffering sigh, Brent agreed.

"And swear to me you will not leave the train at any of the stops."

"Hannah, you're worse than our nursemaid."

"I don't care. I love you more than your nursemaid ever did. I worry because I care. Now promise me."

Maryanne giggled over her older sister's words and quickly agreed. With another heavy sigh, Brent finally agreed, too. "Fine, Hannah, we won't leave the train without you." He perked up. "But maybe you could hurry up and be ready and we could leave together."

"I need to make sure all our things are ready for when it's our stop. Don't press your luck. Be grateful I'm allowing you out of my sight."

Brent glared at her, and she relented.

"Very well. I will try to be quick, but I'm not certain when the next stop is. If I'm not ready, I have your word that you will remain aboard."

"Fine, yes, you have our word."

The two scampered off, and Hannah sank back down onto the bed. While, in a certain way, the travel had been restful, trying to keep up with the two children had been exhausting mentally. She was nervous about the new life she was embarking on, but she was relieved that their travels were coming to an end. Surely, on a farm there would be plenty to keep the children occupied and entertained. And she would get them enrolled in the school as soon as possible as well.

So, she just had to keep it all together until September. With a dry laugh, Hannah rolled her eyes at herself. She shouldn't be wishing her life away.

It felt like the blink of an eye, but the day was passed and they arrived at their stop. Brent and Maryanne had finally caught her nerves and were silently holding her hands as they waited to step down to the platform. Hannah suspected Brent didn't even realize he was doing it because she was certain he wouldn't hold her hand on purpose. The thought made her smile, and she loved him for it.

Looking out over the crowds, Hannah wondered which gentleman was theirs. It seemed there was an inordinate number of men. Not that she had spent much time around the train station in Boston or any of the other cities they had stopped at on the way West, but now that she was standing here, she realized that the further west they had travelled, the higher the ratio of men to women. Now here they were, and she felt decidedly outnumbered.

"Mrs. Delaney?" A deep voice spoke from just behind Maryanne, making the little girl jump and Hannah tighten her hands convulsively. She actually liked the sound of the man's voice, but she had been startled by his nearness. And the unfamiliar name didn't settle her nerves any, either.

Not sure exactly how to respond, she merely smiled and, letting go of Brent's hand, she offered hers to the man to shake. "How do you do?" she asked politely.

"It's a pleasure to meet you," he answered, his wide-set eyes seeming to take in everything as his gaze swept her from the brim of her hat to the soles of her shoes before bouncing over to examine both Maryanne and Brent. "And this must be Brent and Maryanne," he commented. "My name's Ransom. I'm pleased to meet you."

Both of Hannah's siblings remained silent but they seemed to be pleased by the fact that he reached out to shake each of their hands in turn. Brent, always sensitive about his advancing years, was gratified to have a man treat him as more than a child. Maryanne had always been shy, so Hannah wasn't surprised that the child had nothing to say.

"Is your niece with you?"

"Francine wouldn't let me come without her. She's so excited to meet the three of you. But she didn't want to be trampled in the crowd, so she's sitting just behind us in the wagon. I'll just give the porters a hand with your luggage and we can be on our way."

Hannah blinked with surprise as he strode away. She had finally met her husband of one week but was still trying to assimilate her first impression of him. He seemed intelligent and articulate, just as she had surmised from his letter. He was clean, a fact for which she was grateful. That had been one of her deepest fears after encountering a few less savory characters on the train as they had travelled. And he had all his teeth, which was a surprise. Even in Boston, a loss of teeth was a common occurrence.

She had to smile at her own musings. Her mind was tripping around to every subject except to the very first impression she had gained when her eyes encountered his after he startled her with his greeting. He was dreadfully handsome. It was a trifle off-putting. She hadn't expected that. Hannah had rarely set eyes on anyone so good looking. Even the best-dressed gentlemen of fashion in the city didn't hold a candle to her husband, and he wasn't wearing anything of note. Imagine him in a suit, she thought with a shiver. She felt tongue-tied and *gauche* being so travel worn and weary. But she refused to be cowed by something so superficial as her husband's handsomeness. Hannah lifted her chin, held tight to Maryanne's hand, and strode forward in the direction Ransom had indicated when he gestured toward his niece.

Brent had followed Ransom. Hannah wished she had admonished her husband to keep an eye on the boy, but she hadn't wanted to embarrass her brother in front of their new acquaintance. She would have to trust the man would realize his responsibility toward the youngster. Hannah refused to crane her head to keep watch on them.

"Hello there. Are you Francine?" Hannah greeted the small child, marveling that Ransom would leave the pretty little girl by herself. That thought made her want to dash off in search of Brent, but she quelled the impulse. The little sprite was nodding vigorously.

Hannah had to stand on her toes to make proper eye contact with the child in the wagon.

"My name's Hannah, and this is my sister Maryanne. Has your uncle told you about us?"

The child leaned down and threw her arms around Hannah in response. "He said you're going to be my new mama."

Hannah was shocked. She hadn't expected that. She certainly didn't feel qualified or old enough to be someone's mother, even if that was the role she was going to have to fill. The child looked to be about five or six years old. Hannah was surprised the little girl would be willing to accept a new mother if she had only recently lost her own.

"Are you all getting acquainted?" the handsome man asked with a joviality that sounded a little forced.

"We are," she replied with a thin smile, hating the awkwardness of the moment. *But really, what could be more awkward than being married to a total stranger?*

The bustle of necessary activity smoothed over the moment and they were soon on their way.

"I had thought we had packed lightly, but it's a good thing you brought such a large wagon," Hannah finally commented once the silence had started to spread.

"I actually thought you would have more things. I was expecting to have to tie things down as they'd be heaping over the sides."

Hannah laughed. "I didn't want to be too burdened on the trip. More things will be sent to us soon."

Ransom nodded.

"Do you live very far from the train station?" Hannah asked. "You didn't say very much about where you live in your letter."

"We live just outside of a comfortable town about an hour from here. It has everything we might need, but we can easily get to this city, or travel further on the train. It's quite a perfect location, in my opinion. I hope you'll agree."

Hannah smiled. "It sounds like a good spot. I've always lived in Boston, so I'll be glad not to be too isolated. I had tried not to have too high expectations, so I'll be pleased with your home."

"It's your home now, too," he chided her.

She nodded but turned her attention, uncomfortable with the direction of the conversation.

"You mentioned your niece goes to the local school. She seems quite young to already be in school."

"She just turned six. It's the summer break right now, but she started going a couple months before the school ended for summer. It gave her something to do and gave me a break. We weren't used to each other. I think it helped."

"Poor little thing. Losing both her parents suddenly when she was so young."

"You can empathize with her, given your circumstances." His warm gaze showed his sympathy.

"True, but at least I'm an adult. Even Maryanne and Brent are twice her age. And they have each other." She paused for a moment as her heart went out to the little girl. "Had you visited her often when she was growing up?"

"No, I was virtually a stranger to the poor little tyke. But we're getting along just fine now."

Hannah glanced behind at the children, a little uncomfortable to be discussing them within their earshot. She was relieved the youngsters seemed absorbed in their own conversations

"When does the school year resume?" Hannah turned the subject again. Her nerves were getting to her.

"In two weeks."

"That's fortunate timing for us, then. Just enough time to get settled and then they can all start together."

"Will you want to send your brother away to a better school?"

Hannah was horrified at the thought but realized she ought to question his words before reacting. "Is the school truly dreadful? I thought you said in your letter that it was quite good."

"It's not dreadful at all. But not everyone appreciates a one room school house when they've lived in a big city."

"We'll have to see how it goes, I suppose. But no, at this point, I would hate to send him away. I realize that eventually he will need to get a more extensive education than can be offered in a country school, but we need to stay together for at least a few more years."

"You sound remarkably fierce on the subject," he observed, a chuckle sounding in his voice.

"That's because I am. I've sacrificed a lot to keep my siblings together. I'm not going to consider changing that at this point." She then turned to him with judgment. "You aren't trying to get rid of him already, are you?"

Ransom appeared truly shocked by her question. "Not at all. Truly, I was really just making conversation." He held up one hand as though in a conciliatory gesture while keeping the other steady on the reins. "It seems to me that we're both nervous and just talking to fill the empty space. I swear to you, I'm not trying to get rid of any of you. If you will recall, I need you here for my niece. And I recognize you come as a package with your siblings. I wouldn't want to change that. My situation helps me to understand yours." He paused before continuing. "If I'm being completely honest, I'm probably feeling a little guilty, as though I don't have enough to offer you in comparison to the city. So, I was feeling the defensive need to offer you an alternative, if you felt the situation here wasn't good enough for your brother."

Hannah appreciated his honesty. "Since we haven't even seen any of it for ourselves, yet, I promise to reserve judgment. But it would have to be beyond dreadful for me to consider a change before a couple years have passed. I have my reasons for wanting my brother and sister to be far from Boston. A village school will probably suit us perfectly." Hannah felt she had told him all that was necessary for now, so she turned the subject again. "Now, tell me about your home."

"Well, it's our home now," he emphasized with a slight smile. "It's probably a little bit ugly from a female perspective. It's nothing like what you'd find in Boston. But it makes up for it with space. It's quite large, even by frontier standards. We aren't limited by neighbors. We can build as big as we're willing to cut the trees for. We actually have enough bedrooms for each of us to have our own, so there's no need for anyone to be uncomfortable tonight."

"Oh! That's surprising. And somewhat unusual from what we saw from the train. It seemed like every house we travelled past was tiny in comparison to what you're describing."

"Well, I can't promise you that the rooms are huge," he began to protest modestly.

"Maybe not, but it seemed to me that many of the houses the train passed were at most two rooms all together, never mind multiple bedrooms in addition to other rooms."

Ransom shrugged. "You don't have to worry that our house is enormous. It is average in our town. Most of the men have done well for themselves."

Hannah felt her brows furrowing in thought. "It would seem you are well to do, in that case."

"I've done all right."

"Then why did you find yourself in need of a bride through an arrangement?"

"Why wouldn't I? Just because my pockets aren't empty doesn't increase the female population of my part of America."

Hannah burst into laughter suddenly. It felt wonderful to laugh. She felt like it had been eons since there had been anything to strike her humor. As she wiped her eyes, she realized her new husband was looking at her as though she had lost her mind. This caused another fit of giggles to assail her, but she managed to get herself back under control quickly.

"Thank you for that. I haven't laughed in too long. It is a wonderful release. But I do hope you didn't think I was being rude. I wasn't laughing at you. Just the way you described your situation was too funny for my disordered thoughts."

"I'm glad I could be of assistance," he answered a little stiffly.

"Oh, please, don't be offended. You must realize our situation is an uncomfortable one. We still have to get to know each other. And we're married! Aren't you a little nervous about it all? On top of the awkwardness, we have three orphaned children between us."

Ransom finally grinned at her, making Hannah's breath catch at the back of her throat. She had almost gotten used to how handsome he was until then. But the twinkle in his blue eyes and the bright whiteness of his smile in contrast with his tanned skin, it was one more thing about the situation to make her uncomfortable. But she couldn't dwell on it as he was continuing to speak.

"You're quite right. We have a situation on our hands. But you seem to be a reasonable sort. You'll get the hang of it all, I'm sure."

Hannah felt her face furrowing into a frown once more, unsure what he meant by his words. Before she could question him, though, their conversation was interrupted by Francine's plea for attention.

"I'm hungry, Uncle Ransom. Are we almost home yet?"

"Almost, darlin'. It's probably another fifteen or twenty minutes until we reach home. But if you check in that sack under your seat, you'll find some apples you can share with Brent and Maryanne." The little girl scrambled to find the bag, squealing with delight over the treasure trove of food. Ransom continued, "If you're feeling particularly generous, you might want to offer some to the grownups, too," he reminded the children.

With her mouth full, Francine asked, "Do you want an apple, Miss Hannah?"

"I would love one, thank you, Francine." Hannah was glad the child wasn't calling her Mama after what she had said at the train station. And the apples looked delicious.

For a few minutes all that could be heard was the rhythmic clomping of the horses' hooves, the jingle of their harnesses, the rumble of the wheels in the dirt track of the road, and the crunch of the crisp apples. Finally, when her hunger had been somewhat assuaged, Hannah giggled again.

"It would seem we had all been ravenous," she observed. "I didn't think I would hear such complete silence from those three."

Ransom grinned. "Did you not feed yours today?"

Hannah could hear his teasing tone and so did not take offense. "Keeping them hungry was my ploy for control." At his surprised glance, she laughed. "In actual fact, we ate well on the train. I was amazed at what they could accomplish in a moving kitchen. But I think nerves got to the three of us and we didn't have the appetite for much this morning. Now that we've met the two of you, some of the nerves have passed and our empty stomachs made themselves known."

Ransom returned her mischievous smile. "Well, we'll feast tonight, then. I left a roast slowly cooking over coals before we left to collect you."

Hannah felt her eyes widen. "You cook?"

"Of course. Out on the frontier, if you don't cook, you don't eat most of the time. Especially in my early days out here. Of course, in my early days, cooking was actually just propping whatever I had caught over a fire, so it certainly was more function than frills. But now that I have a house and a stove, I've managed not to starve to death. I do hope you know how to cook, though, since I'm certain Francine is getting tired of the five things I know how to prepare."

Hannah smiled. "Hopefully my five things are different than your five things." She didn't bother going into detail about her experience since she didn't actually have a terribly extensive amount of experience. She had watched many things being cooked. And had assisted slightly. Especially when she had been a child. The cook and housekeeper had enjoyed her prattle as she stood on a chair and stirred whatever bowl they were working on. Her favorite thing as a child had been to measure. But Cook hadn't really believed in measuring. She felt that a true baker or chef just knew. Well maybe that was true, but Hannah thrived on precision. And she wasn't about to claim to being a true baker or chef. So, she had forced Cook to write out some of their favorite recipes as closely as she could surmise for what the proper measurements might be. Hannah could envision that there might be some interesting meals in their future while she figured things out. But she didn't want to divulge all of that to her new husband. Her concerns must have not written themselves across her face because he just returned her smile and allowed the subject to drop.

Hannah was finding the drive fascinating. The scenery was beautiful. Of course, she had travelled outside of Boston more than once in her life, but she had never really ventured very far. Her parents had promised her when she had been a child that they would take her to England, but that adventure was put on hold once her siblings were born. Now that they were getting bigger, Hannah had supposed they would finally take that trip, but then her parents, her mother especially, had started hinting they thought she ought to be getting married. Now they were gone. It would seem they would never make the trip now. Especially now that she had moved her family in the opposite direction.

Dragging her thoughts away from the melancholy subject, Hannah returned her attention to the scenery. She hadn't given it a great deal of thought prior to their travels, but she wouldn't have thought the scenery would be all that different. She had been of the opinion that trees were trees, but she had apparently been wrong. The trees here were different than what she was familiar with. And then, of course, the air smelled differently, too. She should have realized that leaving the ocean behind would mean leaving the salty air behind as well. She took a deep breath. The air smelled sweeter. For a moment, she felt a stab of homesickness and she longed for the salty scent, but she forced herself to take another deep sniff and she realized that this was pleasant, too.

Maryanne must have been thinking along the same lines. "It smells so nice here, doesn't it, Han?"

"It sure does."

"It smells green," the little girl commented, making everyone else laugh. "It does smell green," she insisted, sounding irritated. "Like plants instead of water."

Hannah soothed the moment over. "I was just thinking that it smelled sweet because there's no ocean nearby."

"I like sweet."

The little girl's comment made Hannah smile. "I know you do, because you're a sweetie."

Brent guffawed but Hannah kept the peace. "What do you think, Brent? Do you think it smells good?"

Hannah realized her mistake when her eyes met her brother's belligerent gaze. "It smells like manure." Hannah blushed over his words, noticing that the horses had just relieved themselves.

"That happens in the city, too." She kept her comment mild, and he answered her with a shrug.

Feeling too tired to deal with his attitude at the moment, she turned back to face the front, offering her husband a weak smile on the way. "They've faced a lot of changes in a short period of time," she excused.

"I can imagine. Can't be easy for you."

Her eyes wanted to fill with tears at his understanding words but she blinked them away. If she allowed herself to weep now, she might never stop. She was grateful he had mentioned they were almost there; she didn't think she could manage the motion of the wagon for much longer. They had been in almost constant motion for a week, and she hadn't sat still for more than a moment in the couple of weeks before getting on the train. Hannah was longing to sit in a chair and sip a cup of tea and not feel the steady movement of wheels beneath her for at least a month. Of course, she had to fill the role of mother now. She doubted there would be much sitting about in her future. She tried not to mind.

"There it is." She could hear the note of pride in his voice as Ransom pointed to the roof that was now visible above the tree line ahead of them.

"You weren't exaggerating," she commented. "It does seem quite large."

"It will be perfect for our needs," he returned, a note of defensiveness in his voice.

"You're quite right." She agreed with him, although a part of her was dreading the thought of having to keep such a large house clean and dust free. She would have to ensure the children were trained to share in the tasks. She had no intention of doing it all herself. If worse came to worse, she would figure out a way to hire some help. It wasn't as though she couldn't afford it.

That last thought fortified her spirits and she was able to look forward almost eagerly, anxious to see her new home.

Chapter Five

Ransom tried to see everything from his new wife's perspective. He had told her the house was a little ugly. It wasn't a lie, except that she might think it was very ugly, he supposed. He ought to have painted it. But he kind of liked the dull grey it had settled into with the passage of a little time. And he certainly liked how the windows all seemed to twinkle in the sunlight. Ransom was proud of those windows. It had taken some doing to get all the glass here in one piece. Even his neighbors with bigger houses didn't have more glass on their houses than he did. He loved the view from the spot he had chosen for the house. He wanted to be able to see it from every room. Of course, you couldn't see that same view from the back of the house, but it wasn't such a bad view there either.

He was a little disgruntled with himself for how nervous he was to show his bride the place. Since he didn't even know her, her opinion shouldn't matter to him so much. But she was beautiful and seemed intelligent, and well, he had married her. He wanted her to like it here. Heaven knows she was going to be stuck here, so he hoped she didn't hate it too badly.

Casting a glance toward her out of the corner of his eye, he noticed the serene look on her face. She wasn't smiling, but she wasn't frowning. He had noticed she looked like that when she stepped off the train. She was such a striking woman — he had noticed her right away. She looked more mature and serious than he had expected for a twenty-year-old woman. He supposed her circumstances had forced that upon her. Maybe having much younger siblings had also made her grow up fast. Not that twenty was so very young, he reminded himself. Wilbur Channing from across the glen knew first hand just how old twenty could be. His wife had died in childbirth before she turned twenty. They had already been married for more than a year when that happened.

Ransom liked the look of his wife. Her eyes reflected intelligence. He liked how they lit with laughter even when she kept her face straight. She did that especially when the children said something. It seemed she was conscious of not wanting to hurt their feelings. *That's a woman for you,* he thought, *always concerning themselves with feelings.* It's exactly why he needed a wife so quickly. He couldn't be expected to deal with Francine's feelings. And the little tyke seemed to have lots of them. Very few of which made any sense to Ransom. He was thrilled to be able to hand that responsibility over to his wife.

There were so many responsibilities he was going to be handing over to her. He glanced at her again. Underneath that ugly hat brim she really was quite beautiful. She was going to draw attention.

"Do you know how to shoot?"

She was obviously not expecting this question. "Shoot what? A gun, do you mean?"

"Yes, do you know how to shoot? Have you ever handled a gun?"

"No, I have not."

The look on her face led Ransom to believe she wasn't terribly interested in starting, so he averted his eyes as he replied to her.

"I'll teach you how before dark."

"Is there a particular reason why you feel such urgency in my learning how to handle a gun?"

Ransom wanted to smile over how her words became more high falutin' when she was trying to hold onto her emotions.

"It's dangerous around here sometimes. I want you to know how to protect yourself and the little ones."

As she studied him, Ransom grew uncomfortable under her scrutiny but bore up under it. He didn't know what she was searching for on his face, but he wasn't about to tell her at this moment.

"I don't like the idea of guns, but you're quite right that I need to know how to protect the children."

He noticed she didn't mention protecting herself and wondered at her selflessness. He hadn't thought too much about what type of woman would be accepting his offer of marriage by proxy. Now he was filled with all sorts of questions. But he would have to ignore his curiosity for now.

Before he could get too worked up about it, they pulled into the yard between his house and the main barn. He looked back at her to see her reaction, but once again she had that pleasant, non-expressive look on her face. He was beginning to hate that. He didn't know her very well, of course, but it seemed to him that she pulled a mask over her face whenever she didn't want to reveal her thoughts. It was probably a useful skill, he marveled, but it was one he would prefer she didn't possess. *She would make a great poker player,* he thought with wry amusement.

The children were scrambling down despite her admonitions to be careful. Ransom was amused at the way her siblings ignored her words. Francine hesitated in her mad dash from the wagon, but ultimately the lure of older children was too strong and she hurried after them, eager to show them her domain. Turning to his bride, Ransom offered her his hand to help her climb down from the high seat she was on.

He was again tempted to laugh at the struggle that flitted across her face before she smoothed out her expression once more. Ransom could tell she didn't really want to touch him, but she had the sense to realize that it would be much easier to get down with some assistance. She didn't quite know how to maneuver out of the wagon, but her natural grace took over and she managed to get down without mishap, quickly dropping his hand as soon as her feet touched the ground.

"Thank you," she murmured politely, keeping her face averted in a fruitless attempt to hide the heat of embarrassment from him.

"You are quite welcome." He didn't want her to think he was laughing at her, so he quickly changed the subject. "Was that apple enough to tide you over for a little while so I can show you around, or would you like to go in right away and prepare dinner?"

She looked slightly horrified at his words, and Ransom realized she probably thought he was planning to ensconce her in the kitchen immediately. That had not been his intention, but he wasn't sure how to recover his words. He had meant that he would finish the preparations. After a week of travelling, he was certain she must be exhausted, especially while in the company of her brother and sister, who no doubt had required a great deal of entertainment or at least monitoring. Feeling awkward, he waited to see how she would respond.

It seemed to him that she was choosing her words very carefully. "I am not ravenous, thank you for enquiring. I would love a tour of your property."

"Our property, now," he reminded her before adding, "We cannot tour the entire property as our lands do extend pretty far back, but I will show you around what's nearby here."

"How far back does it go?"

"About a mile." Ransom tried not to sound too proud, but he loved his land.

"Really? How do you maintain it all?"

Ransom had to laugh. "We aren't in a city, so it doesn't all require maintenance. Some of it is merely forest. It's where I got most of the wood for the house. The rest is fields for the cattle."

"Do you have a large herd?"

He was happy that her questions revealed a degree of knowledge, surprising for a girl so clearly from the city. "Enough for our use and some to sell. I don't concentrate on farming or ranching. But they serve our needs."

She nodded but didn't appear to fully understand his words, however he didn't feel like telling her everything at that moment. She would find out soon enough. He led her to the barn while his ranch hand hurried out of it.

"Welcome home, Delaney," the man greeted him with a hand to the brim of his hat while his curious gaze remained glued to Hannah. Ransom felt his ire rising even though the man was his friend.

"Scott, meet my wife. Hannah, this is my right-hand man around here. Scott Cooper. He'll be happy to lend you any assistance you might require." Ransom could here himself getting stiff by the end of his speech. He avoided Scott's gaze.

"It's a pleasure to meet you," Hannah replied with sweetness, offering her hand to shake.

Scott grinned, shaking her hand and glancing at Ransom to enjoy his discomfort.

"The horses could use your attention, Scott," he reminded.

"It was a pleasure to make your acquaintance, Miz Delaney," Scott declared as he walked away.

Hannah turned her attention back to Ransom. "Do you have much hired help?"

"Only Scott," he answered. "As I said, while I love the land, it isn't my primary concern, so we just do enough to fill our needs and have a little extra to share or sell."

"That seems generous of you."

Ransom enjoyed her tone of approval. He doubted it would remain long, once she heard of his plans. He took her into the barn. "This is where we keep the horses. The cows mostly stay in the pasture. There's another barn for them further back."

"So, your cows are only for meat?" she asked. "Not for milk?"

"We can get some milk from them for our own needs, if we choose. We've been needing it more since Francine came to live here, and I suppose you'll want some, too, but previously, I just took enough from them to add to my tea or coffee."

He was surprised by her quick smile. "Oh, I'm glad to hear you drink your tea and coffee like a civilized person! On the train, they were surprised I asked for milk for my tea. It had me worried."

Ransom smiled at her words. "Totally civilized, I promise you." He continued the tour.

"We have hens over here. They happily provide us with eggs as well as meat when they are no longer able to produce."

"Does Francine have a problem with that?"

"No, but she's young. Your brother and sister might if they've never really thought about where their food comes from."

Hannah nodded. "I didn't think to talk to them about it." She sighed but then tried to cover it up. "I will cross that bridge another day."

Before long, Ransom had showed her everything he thought she needed to know except how to shoot. He glanced toward the sun. He figured there would be enough daylight after they had eaten. She was starting to look a little worn out and it would be best if she weren't completely exhausted when he taught her.

"Let's head to the kitchen now. You can keep me company while I finish preparing our meal, or you can start your unpacking if you would rather."

She moaned slightly. "I would rather ring for a maid," she said with a laugh before following him to the kitchen. "I think the unpacking will have to wait. I'm relieved to see that your home seems to be in quite a good state so I can ease into my responsibilities here. Thank you for that."

"Again, it's our home," he reminded her, trying to hold onto his patience. He needed to eat or his mood would sour completely. "Why don't you go ring the bell on the porch? The children will need some time to get in and clean up."

His wife looked surprised at the concept but did as he bade. It only took a minute before Ransom could hear the bell. The first strike was tentative but then she got the hang of it and rang with zeal.

"That is spectacular," she declared with a grin as she stepped back into the house. "I'm not sure if Maryanne and Brent will know what it meant, but I would imagine they could hear it even from quite far away."

"If they haven't abandoned Francine, she'll make sure they know what it meant. You did well with it."

Her smile remained broad. "I think it will be an excellent way to relieve any tensions I might be feeling before the family assembles for meals."

Ransom laughed but then warned, "Be sure you don't abuse it though. It needs to be understood that the bell means to come straight away."

Now it was her turn to look annoyed. "Well of course, I wouldn't abuse it. But if I've had a rough day, you might be called quite vigorously."

Ransom found that he quite liked her sense of humor. He hoped she would be able to hold onto it after the morrow.

The children arrived in a tumult of noise and energy, wanting to fill Hannah's ears with everything they had seen, but she quickly organized and tidied them and before long they were all sitting around the table. Ransom was filled with satisfaction. His house had needed filling.

The meal passed quickly. Hannah insisted on cleaning up.

"It's only fair since you cooked. Before long the children will be able to take over this duty, but for tonight, I will do it."

Ransom hid his amusement at the dismay written across the children's faces at her words, but he allowed her to take away his plate while he sipped his tea. The children scampered off to look through the house, Francine hurrying to keep up with her new, bigger companions.

In moments, Ransom was ushering Hannah back outside after telling the children to remain in the house.

"Can this not wait for a few days? I really haven't seen anything that could be so very dangerous that I would have to shoot it."

Ransom could hear the fatigue and complaint in her voice, but he remained firm.

"No, it cannot wait." He didn't elaborate.

Despite her fatigue and disquiet around the weapon, Hannah was a bright, fast learner. Ransom felt his breath hitch as he put his arm around her to adjust her stance. She was a beautiful young woman, and she smelled like sunshine despite her seven days of travel. His attraction toward her grew, but he ignored the sensation.

He ignored too how adorable he found it when she bit her lip and scrunched her nose as she tried to sight down the barrel as he had instructed. "Don't forget to keep the butt firmly against your shoulder or you'll get quite a kick."

She adjusted her stance once more, sighted again, then pulled the trigger as he had taught her. She shouted with glee and did a little dance as the pumpkin on the fence post fell over.

"I did it!" she shouted while rubbing her shoulder.

"It was a very large pumpkin and you only skimmed the side, but it's better than I did on my first try."

Hannah laughed. "Were you five?"

Ransom laughed with her, appreciating her humor and humility. "No. Seven."

"Well, I really doubt I will find the need to be shooting at anything. Could we not just agree that it is to be your assignment?"

"If I'm around, I will gladly defend you with all that I have. But if you are here on your own, it will be your responsibility to protect the children. And yourself."

"But from what will I be protecting them?"

"You cannot expect me to be tied to your apron strings at all times."

He could see that she was getting flustered. "Well, no, of course I don't expect you to be by my side every moment, but I really don't like the thought of needing to shoot anything. Are there really so many dangers about?"

Ransom shrugged but could see that did not please her. "I've never had a woman on the property. Surely you must realize that a beautiful woman such as yourself could draw unwelcome attention."

Now her eyes were huge and horrified. "You aren't actually trying to say that you would expect me to point that thing at a person, are you? I thought we were possibly talking about bears or something."

"Bears are a distinct possibility."

"I have to say, I don't have much experience in the matter of bears, but I would think they aren't too partial if you're male or female."

Ransom raised his eyebrows in question.

"You mentioned my needing to know how to shoot is because you've never had a woman here before," she explained, her tone revealing her exasperation. "That leads me to think your expected threat is human rather than animal." When he didn't answer right away she added, "I have to say, you aren't really inspiring me with confidence in the wisdom of my choice to head West. I feel like my brother and sister and I would have been safer staying in Boston and facing the wolves there. At least I knew what I was up against there."

"I apologize, Hannah. I didn't mean to scare you with this exercise. I don't know what kind of threat you might face, and I need to know you can protect yourself. It's my responsibility to make sure you have the tools you need to make your way successfully."

She tilted her head and gazed at him with intelligence shining in her eyes. Ransom had to work at not squirming under her examination.

"I'm trying to decide if you are being literal or philosophical," she finally stated. "But this discussion will have to wait for another time. I am about to fall over with fatigue, and I'm almost certain my aim will not be improving until after I have slept. If you could just tell me where you keep the blasted thing, I will try to practice some other time when I know the children aren't likely to be about."

"This one stays by the door."

"By the door? In the house? Are you sure that's wise with children in the house?"

"Where do you think you would like it to be if you find you are in need of it? Would you like to run to the barn when there's a threat on the porch?" His questions sounded sarcastic, but he hadn't meant them to be.

"Do you not have solid locks on your doors?" she countered.

Ransom took a deep breath. She was right; she was too tired for this. She would realize soon enough why he had needed to show her this tonight.

"Never mind about this now. As you said, we need some sleep. I will see you in the morning."

Again, she gazed at him assessingly for a moment before she nodded her head. "Good night, Ransom."

Ransom allowed his gaze to follow her as she made her way toward the house. He was pleased with her and believed she would be excellent for Francine. She was such a dainty, graceful little thing. His eyes narrowed. He supposed she wasn't so very little. It was just in comparison to his own great height that she seemed thus, but he remembered as he had his arms around her demonstrating the proper stance for holding the gun that she had fit perfectly within his hold. His stomach clenched at the memory but he forced himself to ignore the attraction. She would hate him soon enough. If he survived, he wasn't certain if they would be able to salvage a real marriage from the situation, so he shouldn't let his feelings get all stirred into the quagmire.

Feeling positive that he had done all that he could to leave his responsibilities in good hands, Ransom checked that the doors were locked tightly as she had mentioned and made his way to bed. Tomorrow would dawn early before a long day.

Chapter Six

"Where are you going?"

She stood at the counter with a towel in one hand and the cup she was drying in the other. Ransom liked her domestic look as one ringlet she must have missed with her pins slid onto her shoulder. She looked gentle and comfortable in his kitchen. But her tone was confused. He had just tried to tell her goodbye, but she hadn't really been paying attention. She had obviously thought he was just leaving the house, perhaps to the barn for chores, until she had spotted the satchel in his left hand. The left hand that now sported the shiny gold ring she had brought him from Boston. She had given it to him the night before, explaining it had been her father's. Ransom should have thought of rings. Guilt had assailed him, but he ignored it.

"I'm leaving. I have to be in Oregon by Sunday. Monday at the latest."

"Oregon?" She was blinking at him like a baby owl. It would have been cute if he didn't realize that she would be furious when she finally realized what he was saying. "You're going away? To Oregon? A few days away? You're leaving today?" Her voice was rising as she spoke.

"I have a claim out there. I was doing quite well with it when I got word that my brother had died. I've been back here looking after Francine until you could get here."

"Why the urgency? Why didn't you take her there with you? Why don't you take us all there with you? Fred mentioned you had business you had to take care of, but he didn't say it would be immediately. Why would you leave the day after we've arrived?" There was a pause. "That was why I needed to learn to shoot. You realize you're being a deserter, but you don't want me left completely unprotected."

"You aren't completely unprotected. Scott will be here."

"So, you're leaving your brand new wife in the care of another man?" She was incredulous. "That sounds like a recipe for disaster."

"Fred has assured me that you're a reliable woman."

"I am. But I was not provided with a reliable man, apparently." She huffed. "Have you told the children or were you planning to leave that task to me?" Her eyes were widening in horror. "Tasks. I don't even know how to do anything! You're leaving me in charge of a house, three children, and a farm? Don't you realize I was a socialite in Boston? My parents died a month ago. Until I got on the train to come here, I had maids and a butler and a cook and all sorts of hired help. I don't actually know how to do anything useful, and you're leaving me here to fend for myself and care for three children?" Her voice was no longer rising. It had reached the point where she was marveling at the situation. As though she thought she were in a bad dream.

Ransom had suspected she was from a wealthy background when she stepped down from the train. When Fred had telegrammed him about Hannah, he hadn't provided a great many details. Ransom had trusted Fred's judgment and expected an experienced woman to be sent to him. He knew she was intelligent and was certain she'd be able to figure everything out. He didn't have the luxury of time to stay home and help her settle in. He needed to catch the next train heading further west.

"You probably shouldn't have taught me to shoot," Hannah noted, her voice turning cool as her emotions settled deeper into anger. "I hadn't thought I would ever be willing to point that gun at a person, but I'm beginning to think that if I ever see you again, it'll be through the sites of that thing."

Ransom wanted to laugh but restrained the impulse. She was beautiful in her ire. But he had to go.

"I'm sorry that it is so sudden. And I'm sorry there hasn't been time to explain it all to you. But I need to be on the train. Scott is driving me to the station so none of the horses are left there. I'm sure you will be fine here."

"I just don't understand why you've done this. I could've married someone else. And you could've left Francine with a neighbor. Why did you marry me if you knew you would be leaving right away? It just doesn't make any sense."

"I needed to marry someone so that if I don't come back, all that I've worked for goes to someone." He could see that he had caught her attention firmly now. She was still staring at him in horror, but she was no longer blinking like an owl. Her wide-eyed gaze was glued to him. He continued his explanation. "If something happens to me, Francine is yours, and all that I own is yours. You will care for her. I can already see that about you. You will not shirk your responsibilities. You've proven that in what you were willing to do to protect your siblings."

"But I thought I was gaining a partner that would help me, at least for a few days." Her voice was calm as she made her statement, but Ransom could hear despair in her words. He hated leaving her like this but he had to go.

"I'm sorry, Hannah. I've left all the paperwork you might possibly need on the desk in my room. I also wrote down an address to which you can mail any letters you might want to send me. I will try to be back as soon as I can, but it might be a few months."

"A few months," she repeated dully. "A lot can happen in a few months. I could burn down your house and barn and move away with your niece somewhere you'll never find her. Have you thought how she will feel about being left with a stranger? Have you thought about what it will do to all the children's feelings to be abandoned again so soon after their previous losses? What about Francine? Are you not even going to say goodbye to her?"

Ransom ignored the guilt her words caused. He couldn't think of the sweet child's feelings. He had waited long enough. He had to go. If he waited to try to stay goodbye to the child, he knew he wouldn't be able to do it. Ransom was actually glad that the children were already outside. He wanted his departure to be as easy as possible.

"I don't have a choice, and I don't have time to discuss it any further."

"Discuss it any further? But you haven't discussed it at all!"

Ransom was beginning to get frustrated with the woman. *What did she think I was going to do? Change my plans just because she doesn't like them?* That couldn't happen. He needed to be on that train. He had waited as long as he could. She was here now, she had agreed to be his wife, she needed to take over here so he could go and look after what needed to be done.

He picked up his satchel and walked to the door. Before he walked through it, he looked back at her. That was a big mistake. His heart paused and his stomach clenched. She looked so beautiful and bewildered as her eyes filled with tears, but she was trying valiantly to keep them from falling.

"I'll write to you, I promise," he vowed.

"I don't promise that I'll write to you," she answered. "I don't even promise that you'll be welcome to return. I'm not even sure if our marriage is legal if you're leaving so soon." He realized her words were merely bravado. She was trying desperately not to be afraid. He felt like the worst heel for leaving her so suddenly and could imagine it was devastating. As she had said, she didn't know anything about his place or his niece. He ought to try to reassure her.

"Everything is legal, I checked. I'll try to be back quickly."

"Is there nothing I can say to change your mind about leaving?" she asked, her voice small and hesitant.

Ransom felt as though he were kicking a kitten as he answered her. "No, this needs to be done. I'll be in touch," he added as he opened the door and strode out. He had been so anxious to go, it shouldn't be difficult to do so, but a part of him wanted to stay behind and get to know his new wife, comforting her in her grief for her parents and whatever the situation was that had made her accept his proposal. He knew he was leaving her in an awkward position, but he couldn't see a way around it. He needed to catch the train.

Without another backward glance, he climbed up onto the seat of the waiting wagon, grateful that Scott had gotten it ready at the appointed time.

"You were slower than I expected leaving the house," Scott commented. "Taking a loving leave from the new missus?" he teased.

"I don't want to talk about it." Ransom knew his words sounded like a growl, but he couldn't put it politely at the moment.

He didn't want Scott thinking they weren't a loving couple even though he knew they had only met the day before. Hannah's words about leaving her with a hired hand had struck him. Scott wasn't an ugly man. And while he was a loyal friend, Hannah was a beautiful woman who would be looking for someone to lean on in the coming weeks.

"Are you sure you're going to be comfortable staying on with her while I'm away?"

"There's nothing for me to be uncomfortable about," Scott answered, seeming confused by the question. "Are you feeling uncomfortable about me sticking around?"

Ransom shrugged and Scott laughed.

"You don't want to leave your beautiful bride behind. You're having cold feet about leaving her, aren't you?"

Ransom shrugged again. He thought Scott was going to fall out of the wagon he was laughing so hard at Ransom's expense.

"I really don't see the humor in this situation."

"Of course, you don't," Scott agreed when he managed to regain his composure. "Listen, Delaney. You and I are friends. You married her. She's your woman. You can trust me with her. I will stick by her to help with the heavy chores, just like I would do for you. I expect you to pay me, of course," he added with a grin. "But I'll do my best to protect your wife and the youngsters from whatever threats you might be fretting about." He paused and they both stared out at the passing landscape, deep in thought. "I do recommend you hurry back as quickly as you can, though. If word gets out that you've left a beautiful woman behind, things are bound to get ugly."

Ransom grunted in agreement. He hadn't expected her to be so lovely. He should have asked her a little more about her own situation. Why she had agreed to their arrangement. But he had been so relieved to have a wife to take over his home; he hadn't given too much thought to her motivations. He knew she was running from something. That marriage was a protection for her in some way. But he didn't know the details. He ought to. But if he knew, he'd probably feel even worse for leaving her. He would have to hope that being legally wed would be protection enough for her for now. And he would hurry as Scott had admonished.

It wouldn't even be a hardship. It had only been one day but already, having a wife in the house had made a difference. He hadn't minded being away from his place before. Long stretches could pass when he wouldn't even think about his land, knowing Scott had it in hand, he didn't concern himself with it, knowing it was there for him to return to when he was ready. Now, it held a great deal more appeal. But he needed to tie up his loose ends before he could settle in there playing house with his ready-made family.

Ransom shook his head. He had a wife and three children. It was a little daunting. While he felt badly about leaving her so suddenly with all the responsibility and no experience, Ransom wasn't actually all that disappointed about leaving the responsibility behind with her. He had felt overwhelmed with Francine. And now there were two more children. Orphaned children at that. Ones with all sorts of emotional needs that he had no way of filling. No, it was actually much better that it all be left in Hannah's hands. She had seemed capable this morning as she served up a delicious breakfast and dealt with the children and their myriad questions. They'd all be fine without him.

He was pretty sure he was protesting too much, even within the confines of his own head. Ransom reminded himself of what he had been discussing with Scott. Oh yes, things might get ugly when word got out that he had left town and there was a beautiful, young wife alone in his house.

"I trust you'll keep yourself visible if trouble comes knocking."

"Of course. But I'm only one man."

"The town isn't so very wild," Ransom offered. "I'm sure she'll make friends with the neighbors and they'll come to her aid if she needs anything."

"Probably."

Scott didn't seem inclined to discuss it much longer, and Ransom was happy to lapse into silence once more. He would be on the train heading northwest within the next couple of hours. He only hoped he hadn't delayed his departure so long that it wasn't even worth his trip. He hadn't realized, when he had come home after he had gotten word that his brother had died, that it would be months before he would be back. He hated the thought of leaving his mine unattended for so long. He didn't think word had gotten out that he'd had a strike, but one could never be too sure about these things. He hadn't been able to sufficiently secure it before he had left. Ransom had thought he would only be gone a couple weeks at the most since he hadn't known about Francine. Well, he knew she existed, of course, he just hadn't given thought to the fact that he was the only living relative left for her to go to. And he just couldn't allow her to go into an orphanage, as much as that idea had appealed in a certain way.

Even now, as Hannah had suggested, why hadn't he sent her to stay with one of the neighbors? As Scott had mentioned, the neighbors were fine folks. Someone would've surely taken the girl in while he was away. But the child needed a family. He, even as a boy, had hated the fact that he and his brother had no one except each other. He couldn't do that to his niece. He needed a mother for her. And the fact that she would have siblings to grow up with was even better. Ransom didn't care that they weren't actually related. They were connected through Hannah, and he was sure they would be a family. He didn't know how to be a part of a family, but he knew he wanted one for Francine. If he survived this trip, he would learn how to be a part of a family when he got home.

The thought warmed him and he had a smile on his face when the train came into view. It was all going to work out. He was just in time for the train. Already the steam was pouring out and the whistle was blowing. He had bought his ticket the day before while he waited for Hannah and the children, so all he had to do was shake Scott's hand, grab his satchel, and climb aboard.

When he made a quick stop at the post office out of habit, he was surprised to see there was a letter awaiting him. It must have come on yesterday's train and not been sorted by the time he had left. He couldn't help smiling. It was from Hannah. Little did she know, it didn't arrive before she did. He tucked it into his pocket and stepped up onto the train just as it began its slow departure from the station. With a wave of his hat to Scott, he stepped away from the door and went to find a seat.

Ransom got comfortable and opened his letter, surprised at the level of anticipation he felt at seeing her tidy script.

Dear Mr. Delaney:

I feel silly writing this letter but I wanted to introduce myself even though by the time you read this we will already be married. My brother and sister and I will be getting on the train as soon as it can be arranged. I'm sure Fred has already told you all about us but I just wanted to thank you personally for the arrangements you are offering us.

We have lived all our lives in Boston so it will be a bit of an adjustment for us to get used to living elsewhere but we are looking forward to the adventure of it. Well, I should say that I am. My siblings are understandably apprehensive. It will be maybe a little too much change for them all at once, but I have my reasons for wishing to get them away from Boston at this time. I'll explain all of that to you when we meet. Just please understand that you are helping us out immensely through this marriage.

While we will be strangers, I will do everything in my power to learn to be a suitable wife for you. You might have to explain to me what that entails, in your opinion, but I will do my best.

Ransom had to look away from the page for a moment. She sounded so very earnest. Clearly, when she wrote this, she hadn't realized that his ideal wife would be remaining behind to look after his niece while he went off on his adventure. He thought he had been clear with Fred. He looked back at the letter.

I have heard fascinating things about Nebraska and I look forward to seeing it for myself. I also look forward to meeting you and your niece and seeing your home. We should be there shortly.

Yours sincerely,

Hannah Bowman Delaney

Chapter Seven

Hannah stared at the closed door. What had just happened? Her brand new husband of one week, that she had only met the day before, had just walked out on her. With no explanation. It was not as though she had been nagging him or something. She was almost certain it had nothing to do with her. It couldn't be that he had found her lacking in some way since he hadn't even taken the time to get to know her at all. So surely it couldn't be her fault. Could it?

She sank down into a chair and looked around the large room. She felt as though she were in a daze. How was she going to handle this? She took stock of the situation as she looked around some more, forcing her mind to break out of the fog it was in.

It was a large, comfortable house. Not as luxurious in hangings and furnishings as their home in Boston but nearly as spacious. The rooms were larger, there were just fewer of them. But that would be just fine out here on the frontier. She doubted they would have any need for a ballroom here. And in a certain way she found the wooden structure warmer than the stone edifice they called home in the city. She wasn't sure if it would be warmer in actuality when winter arrived, but it was certainly more inviting. There was something imposing about their house in Boston. This house, despite its size, was welcoming, even though she didn't love the dull gray color of the exterior. Perhaps it could be painted.

She laughed, hearing hysteria in the sound. She was thinking about painting the house when she had just been abandoned with three children in the middle of nowhere. And she didn't know how to paint. She must have lost her mind somewhere along the way.

With a start, Hannah stood up and went toward the doorway. Ransom had said he would store the gun by the door. Suddenly, she felt the urge to confirm it was there. Sure enough, leaning against the doorframe, there was the gun. As she checked to see if the gun was loaded, Hannah was torn. Dreadful accidents could surely occur. But then again, of what use would an unloaded gun be in a real emergency? Spying the ammunition on a small shelf above the door, Hannah reached up toward it. She could just reach it if she stood on her toes. Which meant that the children couldn't reach it. Not even Brent, yet. Probably before long he would sprout up and be taller than her, but for now, she was comforted by the thought that none of the children would be able to reach the ammunition without getting a chair to stand on. She would have to practice loading the gun quickly since she would be more comfortable knowing the thing wasn't loaded.

Sitting back down, Hannah marveled at how far her mind had bent in the last month. A month ago, she didn't think of much else than the latest fashions and gossip. Oh, she wasn't trying to disparage herself; she wasn't a total simpleton with nothing going on between her ears. There had been charities she supported, of course. She did good works; her charitable support hadn't just been lip service. But she had never actually been involved with anything of import. But now, here she was, all alone with three children to look after, contemplating the best way to store a gun. *Who was this woman?*

She had been quite happy with who she was before. She had not been one of those girls who felt the need to "find herself." Hannah's life had been on track to being pretty perfect. Then their parents had died, and she had read the Will before the official reading. She was so grateful the lawyers had allowed her that. It had given her a jumpstart on her plans. And she hadn't bothered waiting around for the official reading. Only Uncle Jason would have attended that. She was able to make her arrangements and get the children away from Boston. Of course, her mad dash from Boston had been with the expectation that there would be a reliable, adult male at the end of the journey to help her shoulder her responsibilities.

Hannah realized with a start that she had never relied upon herself alone before. Not even once. Now she would have to learn to do so. Of course, she would expect the children to help. But she would have to direct them. She would have to be the reliable adult for them. Hannah was beyond grateful that they had all gone outside to play while she had been cleaning up from the morning meal and so they were not there to witness her desperate state. She could pull herself together before they came in and she would have to explain the situation to them.

Poor Francine! Hannah would have to explain to the little girl that her only living relative had just abandoned her. Of course, she couldn't put it like that. She would have to tell her in a way that didn't damage her little heart.

With a sigh, Hannah stood up to finish cleaning the kitchen. Even in a catastrophe, the chores still needed to be completed. Then she would have to find some paper and start making lists. As she put away the dishes a part of her wanted to throw them across the room. She was quite sure there would be a certain satisfaction in listening to the crash because it felt like that was what was happening to her life, and she wanted it to be outside of herself, not inside. But she was the reliable adult, she reminded herself, fighting the urge. She couldn't risk the children coming in while she was having her fit. She would have to relieve the pent-up frustration in some other, preferably more productive, way.

Hannah dithered outside Ransom's room for some minutes, castigating herself for her foolishness. She had searched the entire house and was disappointed not to have found any paper. He had mentioned to her, just before leaving, that he had left important papers in his room for her. So, he expected her to enter. It was foolish of her to be respecting his privacy. He had all the privacy he wanted wherever he was, she reminded herself as she pushed the door open.

It was a masculine room. It even smelled differently than the rest of the house. Like him. She took a deep breath. She liked it, but she shouldn't. He was a rat, she reminded herself as she shut the door. She didn't want the children to see her in here because she planned on telling them it was off limits. So, she couldn't spend too long in there.

Looking around, she quickly spotted a small pile of papers on the desk in the corner and hurried over. As she passed through the room, she admired its clean lines. He had left it tidy. That surprised her. Neither her father nor her brother had seemed capable of tidying. But then again, they had maids to clean up after them. She never had found out many details of Ransom's background, so she didn't know if he had always had to fend for himself or not. It seemed he must be all alone in the world if he had found it necessary to marry a stranger in order to provide for his niece. But at least, seeing that he could clean his room, it reassured her that Brent would be able to learn.

Hannah shook her head. Once again, she was allowing random thoughts to distract her. She ignored the rest of the room and moved over to the desk wondering if she should read through the papers before she began her lists. Perhaps they would help her to know what to put on her lists, since she didn't actually feel like she knew what she was doing. With a wry twist to her lips, Hannah sat down at the desk. She was becoming comfortable in the room and the window beside the desk provided excellent lighting. Perhaps she would look the papers over.

Ransom had been thorough, she would give him that much. It looked to her like this was mostly legal paperwork pertaining to the land. And there was also his brother's Will leaving the guardianship of Francine to Ransom. Besides what looked to be bank information, Ransom had written out his own Will leaving guardianship of Francine and ownership of everything belonging to Ransom Ellacott Delaney to his wife Hannah Bowman Delaney. Hannah flushed. He had left her everything he owned. And from the paperwork, it would appear that it was quite a lot. He hadn't even divided it up to give some to Francine. She supposed he had been in a hurry. And he had promised her he was coming back. So, this was just a precaution. But still. He had entrusted all that he owned to her. She read over his list of what he was deeding to her once more. He had land in Oregon? He had mentioned a claim. And Fred had said Ransom would be travelling further west. But what could possibly be so important in Oregon that he would leave his family the day after they arrived?

The last item in the pile was an envelope with her name on it. Her heart quickened slightly at the sight of his distinct scrawl, which was a stupid reaction. She couldn't possibly be attracted to the man after he abandoned her so completely and so quickly. Ignoring the ridiculous sensation, Hannah opened the envelope, almost afraid of what it might contain.

Dear Hannah,

I hope you found this before too long after I left. I'm sorry to have left you so abruptly. You must think me the worst sort of cad. And I deserve that, to be sure. But please trust that it was important or I wouldn't have done it.

Hannah almost snorted. Yes, she thought he was a cad. While on the train, she had foolishly thought it would be good to not have an adult around to witness her learning, now that it came to it, she hadn't expected to be abandoned the first day. She shoved the useless thought from her mind and continued to read.

I know I don't even have to ask that you be kind to Francine despite your anger toward me. I deserve it. She deserves better than she has gotten from life. I believe she will get that from you.

In this pile is the paperwork for my bank account in town. Everything that is in it is at your disposal. Please use it however you see fit. Even if that is to pack up the three children and head back East. I would prefer if you don't, but I will understand if you feel the need. I know you aren't used to it here on the frontier and it might not be to your liking. I would appreciate it if you would send me your direction if you will not be here when I return.

I will be in touch.

Sincerely,

Ransom

The rat! Of course, he doesn't have to ask that I be kind to Francine. She is a darling child, and he is completely accurate in saying she doesn't deserve what she has been dealt with a rat for an uncle and being orphaned besides.

Head back East? As if she could. A part of her would love to return to the familiar, especially now with the added responsibility of a third child. And an entire farm, she added to the growing list. But that wasn't an option. She had to keep the children from her Uncle

Jason's clutches. Of course, with whatever money Ransom had left them and her own, she could take the children to a different city. They had passed a few on their way here. But Uncle Jason would expect that. He would never think to look for them on a farm. So, she would have to figure it out. And surely, she was capable. How hard could it be?

~~~

"Isn't Uncle Ransom coming in for lunch? Did you forget to ring the bell?"

Hannah froze and almost dropped the plate she had been washing. It was too soon; she didn't feel ready to face the children's questions. She wasn't over her fury but didn't want to pass it on.

Taking her time turning around, Hannah coughed to clear the lump from her throat.

"Uncle Ransom has some business he has to look after in Oregon. He's going to be away for a little while."

Brent and Maryanne barely looked up from the toast they were finishing, not bothered by the desertion of a man they had just met, but Francine's wide eyes filled with tears.

"But he didn't say goodbye."

"I know, sweetie, but he asked me to tell you goodbye for him. He had to hurry to catch the train."

"But why didn't he say goodbye to me himself? It wouldn't have taken very long. Doesn't he know he should say goodbye?" Francine's tears spilled over, making Hannah's fury toward her husband deepen. But she had to comfort the child. Carefully placing the plate on the counter, despite her desire to throw it,
~~~

Hannah crouched down to be on eyelevel with the little girl.

"The thing is, Francine, sometimes adults don't like to deal with their feelings. I think Uncle Ransom would have been too sad to say goodbye to you, so he decided not to."

"That wasn't very nice." Francine's voice was muffled as she shoved her face into Hannah's shoulder.

"No, it wasn't," Hannah agreed. "When he comes back, you can tell him not to do it again." When the little girl continued to cry, Hannah had to think quickly. "Maybe we'll make it a rule for this family. No one is allowed to leave the property without saying goodbye. Do you think that would be a good idea?"

The little girl lifted her tearstained face and nodded vigorously.

"Very well. It's a rule. I promise I will never leave without saying goodbye."

"I promise, too."

"Very well," Hannah said with a smile and another hug for the child. "Now go wash your face and then all three of you can go back to playing whatever you were doing before lunch."

The little girl seemed mollified and hurried away to do as she was bid. Hannah looked at her brother and sister. Brent still seemed undisturbed, but Maryanne was watching her with worry written on her face.

"Are you sad that he left?"

How do I answer that question, Hannah wondered. "The four of us are going to be just fine together," she said out loud.

It didn't really answer Maryanne's question, but it seemed to satisfy her. All three children ran outside as soon as Francine hurried back into the room.

Hannah watched them leave wishing she could be as carefree and innocent as they were.

~~~

A few days passed during which she discovered just how very hard it could be to look after three children and a farm. Oh, not the farm work itself. Thankfully, Scott had stayed on and did the bulk of the heavy stuff with that. Even the milking. She had tried her hand at it and almost got kicked by the poor cow who hadn't appreciated her clumsy efforts.

Once Hannah had figured out how to collect the eggs from the chickens, she had shown Francine and Maryanne how to do it, and the two girls happily took over that task each morning. Brent had been a little harder to set to work, but he soon started following Scott around, helping him with various chores. When Scott suggested that Brent learn about the garden, there had been no resistance, although he had rejected the idea when it had come from Hannah. Maryanne was enthusiastically sharing with him things she had learned from the large tome she had read on the train.

Hannah didn't hold a grudge. Whatever it took to get the boy involved. She was just glad he was helping out, since she couldn't do it all herself. Just preparing meals was a big chore. She had forgotten that when she had worked in the kitchen at home, there had been an entire staff to assist. She had only had to do one aspect, like chopping, or one dish, like baking a dessert. Here,
~~~

she was the only one. She had to chop, stir, measure, monitor.

She grimaced as she remembered when she had forgotten that last part. Monitoring the progress of the meal was important. Hannah was sitting at Ransom's desk trying to compose a letter to him. She was debating what tone she should take. Should she tell him about her triumphs and failures? Should she tell him anything? Should she even be writing to him? She was living in his house. And even though he didn't know it, he was still providing a refuge for her and her siblings. For that she had to be grateful. And it only felt fair to keep him apprised of Francine's progress. Now that more than a week had passed, so too had the majority of her fury. She felt ready to write a civilized letter.

Dear Ransom,

We are well. I have to tell you, I'm still rather angry with you, but I have come to the conclusion that it isn't really fair of me to remain resentful. Fred did tell me you needed a wife to care for Francine while you went further west. It isn't really your fault I didn't understand it was to be immediately. The children don't seem to note your absence. Francine was upset that you didn't say goodbye, so there is now a household rule that no one is allowed to leave the property without saying goodbye to the other family members. Just so you know for next time.

I didn't burn down the house yet. I didn't even try to do so intentionally, but I thought I had done it by accident. It turns out you really can fill this entire house with smoke despite its size. Your room escaped unscathed as the door is kept shut, but every other room in the house needed to be completely aired out after I forgot about the cookies I was baking and went out to check on the garden.

I wish I could ask you why you planted such a large garden. We are not enjoying the upkeep. To our advantage, we didn't know which things were weeds and which were plants, so the garden isn't as large as you had intended. Perhaps you knew that would happen and planted so much as a form of insurance. Surprisingly, Brent has actually taken a liking to the garden. With their little hands, the children are quite good at weeding. I ask them each to do a little bit each day so we can keep ahead of the task.

You might not have realized this about us or maybe I told you when you were taking your leave, I don't remember that brief period so well, but we had servants in Boston. I didn't realize how very much they did for us. It is an adjustment learning how to do everything for ourselves. Brent and Maryanne objected quite vocally at first, as you can imagine, but are slowly accepting the new order of things. It might help if I explained to them why we have to be here. But I don't want to burden them with that. Anyway, I've thought about hiring help around the house, but I don't want to draw attention to us and I'm sure the neighbors would gossip about the new wife who can't even keep house on her own. And it will surely do us all good to learn how to do things.

The good news is, the children are really looking forward to the start of school. They expect that their chores will disappear when they are occupied with school. I haven't explained to them yet that it isn't likely.

Of course, I will have to lessen their chores, but I won't be able to manage everything by myself. And how fair would it be if I did, anyway? Surely, I shouldn't have to do it all.

Anyhow, this probably has the air of complaint. I'm sorry for that. It wasn't my intention. I just wanted to let you know that we are surviving. I haven't poisoned anyone with my attempts at cooking and none of the children have yet run away from sheer terror. And I haven't yet had to use the gun, although I am getting faster at loading the stupid thing and my aim is also improving. Brent, of course, is much better than I am. We're going to need more ammunition soon.

I don't really know what is involved with a claim, so I can't even make an appropriate comment but I hope your business is progressing successfully.

Sincerely,

Hannah

She wasn't completely satisfied with the letter but she wasn't going to rewrite it. She hated wasting paper. The cost of it had come as a shock. With a smile, Hannah thought about how far her view of finances had changed in the short time she had been on the frontier. Since she didn't want to contact the lawyers for money until she was desperate, she had to hoard the funds she had brought with her. Hannah hadn't yet felt comfortable enough to go to the bank in order to inquire into the extent of Ransom's account. And since she had only met him for one day, even though she had the license to prove their marriage, she didn't truly feel like his wife, so spending his money was a strange thought anyway. So, they would make do with what they had for as long as possible. Which meant no more wasting of paper.

Chapter Eight

Ransom reread the letter for the fourth time, enjoying it more each time. He could almost hear Hannah saying it as he read. He could feel his smile stretching his face. It was his first time to smile since he had left ten days ago. He was exhausted from the heavy work but relieved to have found everything intact. It seemed no one had discovered his mine, so his claim was still safe. He would have to set up security and hire help before he returned to Nebraska the next time.

Ransom looked around for some paper on which he could write a reply. His rough cabin was not very well supplied. Not that he really knew what to say to her. He wasn't ready to tell her why he was in Oregon. Ransom couldn't even explain to himself why he was reluctant to tell her, so he certainly wouldn't be able to explain it to her. But since she had written to him, he ought to write something in return.

Dear Hannah:

I'm thrilled to hear the house is still standing (or at least that it was at the time of your letter writing). I am well. I reached Oregon without incident. It didn't even take three full days. The speed of modern technology is amazing!

I think you would have enjoyed the scenery along the way. I noticed while we were driving from the train station that you had seemed fascinated with the changing scenery. Of course, you might've just been watching the scenery to avoid looking at me, but you had seemed to enjoy it. Between Nebraska and Oregon there are a several changes. The train passes through the Rocky Mountains, which are breathtaking in their grandeur. I hope you will get to see them one day. And the children, too, of course.

Have you continued to manage all right with the children? I trust they aren't giving you too much trouble. Francine, I'm sure, is happy to follow your lead. Your sister, too, seemed a meek child, but I doubt if your brother is willing to follow your direction without comment. Boys of his age can be a challenge. I know I was when I was twelve. The antics my brother and I got up to would curl your hair. I hadn't really thought of that when I left. Did you tell them yet that their chores will continue even after they start school? I'm not sorry I'm going to miss that scene.

My work here is progressing, but I won't be able to leave as quickly as I had hoped. I do sincerely hope to return before winter, though. I don't want to be stuck in Oregon through the deepest cold. This is a beautiful, rugged state. I find myself wondering what you would think of it. Which is foolish, really, considering I don't even know what you think of Nebraska. I'm sure it's going to change swiftly now that the train comes all the way here. I hope you'll get to see it while it is still wild and free.

Take care of yourself,

Ransom

He reread it before sealing the letter. He wasn't quite satisfied with it, but he wasn't sure what else he could say. He wanted to reassure her that he was returning and tell her how glad he was that she hadn't returned East at the first sign of trouble. On his second read through he realized he hadn't even mentioned that. He added a postscript.

Thank you for taking care of our home in my absence.

That would have to do, he thought with a mental shrug. It's not like he could send her hothouse flowers through the post. The best he could do is let her know he appreciated her efforts. And that he would be returning home as soon as possible.

Ransom scratched his head in thought. He had never in his life been eager to return home, even though he enjoyed Nebraska and was proud of the house he had built. He supposed it was the fact that it had always been empty until now so it held far less appeal to return. Now, knowing he had a beautiful wife and the three youngsters there waiting for him, he was thinking of returning. Before, his home had been nothing more than where he went when he didn't have somewhere else to be. Ransom wasn't comfortable with the tug he felt toward home now, so he shoved the thoughts away and got to his feet to head back to his claim.

~~~
~~~

Hannah blew her hair out of her face for what felt like the three hundredth time that day. She was trying to wash the laundry. Her hands had already shriveled up and were starting to hurt. She suspected she had put too much soap into the wash water. That would account for the burn of her skin and the difficulty she was having in rinsing the garments. She should've asked for instructions when she purchased the soap at the mercantile, but she hadn't wanted to embarrass herself or Ransom by admitting her ignorance to the shopkeeper. Which was ridiculous. Ransom wasn't even in the same state as her. How would he even hear about her ignorance, let alone be embarrassed by it? And really, she oughtn't be embarrassed to ask a question. How else would she know if not to ask? Well, she could learn the hard way as she was doing now, she thought with a snort as she yet again blew her hair away from her face.

The hot water she was using for the laundry had frizzled her hair and her vigorous scrubbing had encouraged it to slip from the braid she had twisted it into that morning. Hannah thought longingly of the maids she had left behind in Boston. They would know how to do the laundry with the least amount of fuss. And they would get it done without flooding the floor and themselves with the hot, soapy water, as well. Hannah sighed. There had to be a first time for everything.

She had put off the dreaded task as long as she could, but the children, and she, herself, were running out of clean things and she couldn't allow them to think it was all right to wear dirty clothing. They might be in the middle of nowhere Nebraska, but she couldn't allow them to lose their civilization. Brent especially. He, even more than the girls, would love to turn into a mountain man. But she needed to prepare him to return East. She had every intention of sending him back to attend university, and he would have to be prepared to take over their father's business interests when he was older. He couldn't do that if he became an uncivilized ruffian.

Scrubbing harder, she thought that maybe he could be a ruffian just for the rest of the school break. She shook the traitorous thought from her head with an impatient rattle. She was not willing to live with the stink. The laundry needed to be finished now that she had started it.

Dumping the water out the back door, Hannah was pleased that very little of it ended up on her this time and almost all of it made its way outside. She refilled the tub, marveling once more that there was running water in her kitchen. She hadn't realized that was a luxury until Scott had explained it to her. There was a spring in the hills behind the house so gravity fed the pressure in the pipes Ransom had laid for his lovely house. If not for that, she would have had to pump the water from the well he had shown her before starting the task of laundry.

Technology certainly sped things up, she admired, shuddering to imagine how much more onerous the task would have been. Of course, she could have asked Brent or Scott to help with hauling the water, but Scott, especially, had enough to do without her adding to it. No, this was much better. Well, she admonished herself, let's not get carried away. It's still a dreadful chore, but at least she was saved from carrying the water further than necessary. She still had to dump it each time. And she still had to somehow get all this soap rinsed out of the clothes. And then she had to lug the wet clothes out to the line. She thought longingly of her bed. A nap would be wonderful right about now.

Hannah shoved the self-serving thought from her mind. Napping was not a luxury afforded to the guardian of three children and the mistress of a large house. She supposed she could have enlisted the girls' help, but she remembered so fondly her own idyllic childhood that she wanted to replicate that for the children as closely as possible. Of course, without servants and two parents and money, it was going to be a challenge, but the least she could do was allow them time to play out of doors while they were on a break from school. They had been assigned enough chores. Hannah would do the rest. Even if it killed her. Or ate off her hands, whichever came first.

She started to laugh. None of her friends would recognize her if they saw her right now. She didn't think anyone of her acquaintance would have any more clue than she did how to wash the laundry. She, of course, had asked the housekeeper before she left Boston. But she hadn't been thorough enough in her questions, it would seem. She had been told to add the soap but hadn't asked for a measurement. Hannah blew her hair off her forehead for the millionth time and squeezed out a garment, satisfied to finally see the water running clear rather than bubbling with soap. The task was nearing its end. She made a mental note that laundry would have to be done more frequently as she gazed with a degree of horror at the pile she still needed to deal with.

Allowing her mind to wander to the letter she had received from Ransom when she had gone to the village to shop afforded her a few moments of distraction as her hands continued in their task.

Thank you for looking after our home. Hannah wondered, when she had read that, if he were being sarcastic or not. She hadn't really gotten to know him well enough to know what kind of sense of humor the man had. Or if he had one at all, really. Perhaps he was just being polite. She really liked that he kept insisting that his house and lands were theirs, not his. It helped her feel slightly more married than she felt after having only met him for one day. It also made her more comfortable with rearranging things, or even touching things in the house. She left the majority of the outdoors things to Scott.

Now there was an interesting man. He barely uttered a word. He would nod, maybe even grunt, if she ever spoke to him. Of course, if she asked a direct question, he would be forced to answer her, but he always managed to do so with the least amount of words. It was a fascinating skill.

She, on the other hand, ended up with far too many words whenever she spoke with him. Hannah supposed it was nervous energy on her part that made the words flow like a waterfall from her mouth at awkward moments. She couldn't even pinpoint why the man made her so nervous. She supposed it was Ransom's last words about her safety. And Scott was a large man who would barely speak. Likewise, she was turning into a hermit. Hannah hadn't spoken to anyone except the children since she had arrived.

But Ransom had left Scott here to care for things, so Hannah was trying to trust the man. And he was doing wonders with Brent. Somehow the belligerent boy had taken to the quiet mountain of a man. And she presumed that the man spoke to her brother when she wasn't around. Or they had some mysterious male form of communication. Whatever the case, Brent was settling in to life on the frontier maybe better than any of them. Too well if she thought about it too much, but she would worry about that at a later date. She needed to live with the boy for several years. They couldn't be at war the entire time.

Hannah glanced at the calendar hanging on the wall. They had been here for two weeks. School started in a little over one week. She needed to make sure the children had all the clothing and supplies they might need for the start of school. Who could she to ask about what the children would need? Sighing again, Hannah lamented her shoddy education. She could host a large dinner party or plan a fundraising gala, but she didn't know how to raise three children on the frontier. If she asked at the mercantile, she suspected they would tell her far more than she needed. Perhaps it was time for her to meet her neighbors.

She was actually rather surprised she hadn't been visited yet. Did no one know she was there? Or was it just not a warm community? She had rather thought that people in such isolated places as this would be more involved in each other's lives than they were in the city. But perhaps Ransom had made a habit of disappearing, and the neighbors weren't used to trying to be close to him.

She thought again of his letter and sighed. He had seemed to be genuinely concerned with how she was making out with the children. But obviously not concerned enough to be here to help her. And he had said his work wasn't progressing as quickly as he had hoped. What did that mean? He'll be another week? A month? Several? Would he ever return? What if something happened to him out in Oregon? Would she ever even know? Had he told anyone about her and how to reach her if something did happen?

Hannah realized she was scrubbing too hard in her frustration. Taking a deep breath, she let it out slowly, wiping her forehead and shoving her loose hair off her face once more. There was no need to get herself all worked up. He had obviously thought about the possibility of something happening to him. That was why he had left that pile of paper on his desk. He wanted to make sure she and Francine would be taken care of if he didn't come home. She would be fine. They would be fine. She had barely even met the man, so it wasn't as though she would miss him if he didn't return. But that wasn't quite the case. Being in his home, she felt as though he had a presence here. There were things she could learn about him from being here. He had designed and built this house. It was a strong, sturdy, spacious house. He hadn't built a shack. That told her he didn't do things in half measures and he was a hard worker. He saw things to completion. So, whatever he had to take care of in Oregon, he wanted to see to completion. Could she really fault him for that? She actually appreciated that quality. She would prefer to be on the receiving end rather than being left behind, but such was life. She hadn't been on the receiving end of a good roll of the dice recently.

Really, Hannah assured herself, she oughtn't be angry at the man. She hadn't been led astray. Or if she was, it was her own assumptions. In fact, she knew he was going to be away. On the train ride here she had even been relieved he wouldn't be around to witness her learning mistakes. She was just disgruntled because she was lonely for adult companionship. She really ought to get herself out and make some friends. If she could only figure out how to get everything done and have a few spare minutes to do so.

It could have been worse. Way worse. She had married a man she didn't know by proxy; before ever even meeting him, they were legally bound. While she wasn't thrilled with the fact that he had up and left the day after her arrival, leaving her with an extra child and a large house and property to look after, it could have been so much worse. He could have been a drunkard. Or abusive. Or just hideous in some way. She still didn't know Ransom very well and she was still disgruntled that he left so suddenly with almost no explanation, but he didn't seem to be any of those things. And he had made provision for them. There was a hired hand to take care of the outside things. There was a bank account she was afraid to access, but knowing it was there was a comfort. There was a large, sturdy home that would shelter them. They were safe from Uncle Jason.

She was Mrs. Hannah Delaney. Jason would never find her. She wondered if there was any sort of registration needed for the school. Should she register the children with the name Delaney? A part of her balked at that. She did not want to erase her parents. She didn't want the children to forget the lovely people who had died so tragically. But it would be a protection for them to use Ransom's name. In order to get them to cooperate with an idea like that, though, she would have to explain everything about their Uncle Jason. Her stomach turned over at that thought. She would have to tell them eventually anyway. She couldn't believe they hadn't yet asked more questions about why they had left Boston.

Hannah sighed. Venting her frustrations on the laundry had one advantage, at least. The task was almost done. Her arms felt like they were on fire and her shoulders ached, but all the dirty laundry was now clean and almost all of it was suds free. Her smile felt weak, but she was exultant.

Chapter Nine

Ransom read through Hannah's latest letter one more time. He was going to wear it out at the rate he was going. It was strange how much he was relying on her missives. Strange because he had never really received much mail in the past and certainly hadn't looked forward to it like a child on Christmas day. As it was, he had to prevent himself from going to the post office on a daily basis. It certainly wasn't a productive state. If he enjoyed hearing from her so much, he really ought to concentrate on the matter at hand, finish up his work in Oregon, and get himself back home to Nebraska.

He shoved the paper back into his pocket and stared at the hole in the rock that he was debating about crawling back into. Mining was quickly losing its appeal. With each letter he received from his wife, the less he wanted to be here in Oregon. But if he wanted to keep his wife in a comfortable position, he needed to get as much mining done as he could before the deep cold of winter set in and made it nearly impossible. Once it got cold enough, even if he didn't have everything in place to hire the work out, he would be able to leave without fear of looters or squatters. Then he could go home for the winter and return in the spring. But in the meantime, he wanted to get as much of it done as possible. And really, it was ridiculous that he was feeling such a pull toward a young woman he had barely met.

Yes, her letters were witty and he admired her zeal for the tasks she threw herself into. Like this last letter where she explained how very different everything was from her life in Boston.

When my parents brought my brother home, I thought they were providing me a living doll to play with. It was the very thing I had been begging for. You can imagine how disgruntled I was when they wouldn't let me keep him at my side at every moment. And then when the little monster wouldn't stop crying, I was forced to accept that he wasn't the doll of my dreams. But he has since grown on me. And I'm rather fond of him despite his wayward moods. I'm hoping it's some sort of dreadful twelve-year-old phase and will soon pass. You did mention that you went through something similar when you were his age, didn't you?

Ransom thought back to his own childhood and early teens. He and his brother had been orphaned right about then, just like Brent was. They had been taken in by a much loved uncle, but Ransom could still remember how contrary he had felt, as though he were trying to take out his grief on everyone around him while simultaneously trying to deny that he was even feeling the least bit of sadness. He could feel for the boy. But his heart also went out to Hannah. She had her own grief to deal with and a bewildering amount of responsibility that she had never been prepared for. As she had continued to write about in her letter.

It has been a challenge to adjust to life without servants for the three of us. It seems all Brent wants to do is eat, but I am still learning to cook so that's a rough combination. And then there is the laundry. No one had ever told me that keeping the clothes clean would be such a monumental task. I remember blithely throwing things in the wash because I had worn it for an hour. I can assure you, such habits are no longer acceptable in the Bowman-Delaney household. Not unless the perpetrators wish to take over the task of doing the laundry. Of course, the children don't care overly much about their things. And I don't want them to grow accustomed to filth, so I find myself walking a fine line between keeping them clean but keeping the growing laundry pile to a reasonable height.

Ransom smiled. He could just hear her sarcastic tone as she wrote that, as though she were mocking herself. He liked that about her. She seemed quite sufficiently comfortable in her own skin so as to be willing to make light of herself and her possible failings. He was swamped with a wave of guilt. He shouldn't have left her to flounder so thoroughly on her own. Not that he had any desire to take on the task of laundry. But he hadn't fully realized just how privileged her background had been. It wasn't as though she had grown up helping her mother with the household tasks. She had never done any of those things herself. She had to learn and be solely responsible for them all at once. And she was being so kind as to not want to force the children into servitude along with her. Perhaps he ought to encourage her to hire someone from the village to come in and help her with some of the bigger tasks like the laundry. Then he remembered something she had written.

I've been sorely tempted to send home for the housekeeper or one of the maids. They had sworn to us when we were leaving that they would love nothing more than to come with us. But I'm afraid that would draw undue attention to us. I haven't been able to ascertain if anyone in the village hires help. I have no desire to be the first one to start such a trend. And it would not keep me incognito. Uncle Jason cannot find us. I'm fairly certain Mrs. Hannah Delaney is not the type of woman who hires servants.

Ransom wondered at her wording. It was droll how she spoke of herself in the third person, as though she were figuring out who this person is. He wondered why she was hiding from her uncle. Did he not know she had married? He had so many questions. He really ought to have stuck around a little longer to know her before he had left. But Ransom rather thought he wouldn't have left if he had, with the way he was feeling just from reading her letters.

His distracting thoughts were slowing him down. At this rate, he would have so little done before he had to leave for the winter. He berated himself as he swung his pick once more. Since he had sacrificed so much and abandoned his new family to their own devices, he really needed to make it worth the risk he had taken with his new family. Ransom tried to push all thoughts from his head except where to swing his hammer and pick, taking advantage of what little time he had.

~~~

Hannah stood and watched the children playing. Little Francine was trying so valiantly to keep up with Brent and Maryanne. It was good for her. The child slept like a log every single night, never causing Hannah a moment's trouble. Which was such a relief, as Hannah wouldn't have the first clue how to comfort her. Hannah was impressed with Brent's growing patience with the two girls. She was relieved to note that his belligerent attitude had finally seemed to pass once they had settled here for a couple weeks. She wasn't completely sure what to attribute it to. She thought perhaps the physical labor of working in the garden might have something to do with it as well as Scott's conversations with him about his responsibilities as the man of the house with Ransom away.

Smiling as she watched Brent pushing Francine on the swing they had fashioned from an old length of leather they had found, Hannah allowed her mind to wander over the conversation she had overheard part of.

"Make sure you loosen up all the soil at the roots. Won't absorb nearly enough moisture if you don't," Scott had pointed out while the boy had held his tongue between his teeth in concentration.

Hannah had been amazed at Brent's prolonged interest in the garden. She had expected him to obey her edict to help with the weeding but had thought he would do so with barely concealed disgust. Much to her surprise, after the first day, he had been eager to return to the plot daily. Despite their disastrous first day when
~~~

they'd pulled out more plants than weeds, her brother had taken a liking to gardening and seemed to have a knack for it. If she ever needed to find him, she could usually do so in the large garden patch. Either that or following around after Scott, hanging on his every word.

Scott was adding his lessons about being a big brother to being a gardener. "These little plants are just like your little sisters. You need to help them grow big. If you abandon them to the harsh realities, they'll shrivel up and burn under the sun. That's why we loosen the soil, so the water can get in there gently."

Brent had frowned at the man. "How does that apply to the girls? I can't go after them with a hoe."

The man had laughed. "No, you're quite right about that. I'd go after you with a hoe if you did."

"So, what do you mean?"

"It's your job as their big brother to watch out for them and make things easier for them. It's obvious they think you're the best. If you are mean to them and tell them to leave you alone, they could shrivel up like the plant that can't get any water."

Hannah had marveled how the man had made that connection. She had slipped away not wanting to interrupt, hoping Brent would take Scott's words to heart, but not wanting him to think that she had anything to do with the conversation. She hadn't even thought to seek out Scott's help with the children.

But it was obvious the advice had struck home with Brent. Hannah smiled as her brother laughed along with Francine, who was obviously enjoying the ride as well as the attention of the big brother she was already idolizing. And Scott had been right. The little girl looked just like a flower opening her petals to the sun after a rain. She wondered what sort of a life the child had before coming to Nebraska. Hannah didn't know if asking her about it would do more harm than good. But just like with her brother and sister, she thought all the children ought to talk about their parents even though they had died. They needed to keep them alive in their hearts.

Hannah would think about it a little bit more. She had to be steady in her own mind and heart if she were going to help the children with their grief. She wished she had someone else she could turn to for help in this. With a sigh, she returned to the house. Perhaps she would write another letter to Ransom. Somehow, putting it into words on the paper really helped her, even though the man wasn't there to actually offer her advice. Now that time had passed, she had started receiving responses to her letters, but he was often answering questions she had asked at least a week previously. So it was far from immediate assistance.

Dear Ransom,

The children are getting along well together, which is a relief. Scott told Brent it was his responsibility to be a good big brother and the boy has really taken to the role. They are at peace and Brent seems to be a little less restless than he was. But now I feel that it is time that I try to get all three children to start talking about their respective parents. I wish there was someone more mature and responsible around to help with this. I wish there was more of a parental figure than just me for them. It feels too huge for me. What if I don't do it right? I wish you could answer me.

Hannah sighed, putting down her pen. She wanted to crumple up the paper and start again but she had vowed to not waste the paper, so she needed to continue. Besides, he ought to know what sort of inadequacies she was dealing with. It might motivate him to come home. *Or it might make him stay away,* she thought with a rueful grin. Either way, he would know what he was in for.

Anyhow, whatever I decide, they start school on Monday and there are varying degrees of excitement in the house. Francine is almost beside herself. I'm not sure if it's entirely for school, though. I managed to make her some new dresses. That was an entire ordeal in itself. I thought it would be easy since I know how to do needlepoint. That was self-deception of the worst sort, I must tell you. But the fabric is very pretty and I managed not to lose too much blood in the process, and the dear child is delighted with the end results. I think a large part of her excitement is the fact that I managed to make her hair ribbons to match each new dress. She is a dear.

Maryanne is cautiously excited about school. For her, the new clothing is a walk on the opposite side of fashion from what she is used to, so she is desperately hoping that our trunks arrive soon. I finally gave in and wired my housekeeper in Boston to send the children's clothes. It makes no sense to leave it there since they will outgrow it before there is a chance to return. I just hope Uncle Jason wasn't watching the house, lest he find out our direction. The staff knows to be discrete but it wouldn't be difficult to see trunks being loaded into a carriage, even from the street.

Brent, on the other hand, is dreading it. I have tried to assure him that his plants will be just fine without him to watch them throughout the day. He has done a wonderful job of keeping the weeds at bay and I daresay they can't do much damage with so little time left in the growing season. But as he so succinctly pointed out, I don't know what I'm talking about. He's perfectly correct. I never tried to grow anything in my life. There was a staff member assigned to keeping any plants in the house or on the grounds alive. But thankfully for Brent's education, Scott backed me up and agreed that the garden would be perfectly fine if Brent went to school. Who would have thought the city-bred twelve-year-old would take to country life so soundly? Now I'm beginning to fear I'll never be able to get him to return East for university. But I'll cross that bridge later. For now, whatever it takes to get him to go to any school is worth it. The boy needs to know more than he already does, despite the fact that he thinks he knows everything already. Were you like that as a boy? I'm sure you were a handful then if you're still the sort who needs adventure. I hope it's coming along well and that you are safe.

Take care,

Hannah

<center>~~~</center>

Ransom read the latest letter from his wife and his heart clenched. The young woman was a delight. She was trying so very hard to accomplish everything. He really ought to be there with her, making it at least a

116

little bit easier for her. He should send her a telegram and demand she spend his money and hire someone to do the chores.

When he thought of how beautiful she was when she stepped off the train, it caused his heart to clench and his stomach to hurt at the thought of her doing manual labor. Her hands had probably never felt a callous in their entire life. Now she was probably losing a layer of skin after that laundry episode. Or rather, it had probably grown back by now, since it took so long for him to get his mail. He ought to go check more frequently but he really was trying to get everything done quickly so that he could return to his family.

Ransom laughed as his gaze travelled over the wilderness that surrounded him. He was sitting on an outcropping of rock. From his vantage point, all he could see were mountains and trees. Normally this was his favorite spot on earth. He had even envisioned building a house here. But now, all he wanted to do was get back to Nebraska and see what Hannah was doing to his house. He could just imagine that it must smell and look differently from what he knew. With four people living in it, it must even sound differently.

He chuckled, thinking of a story she had written him about burning an entire meal. That would certainly have affected the scent of the house. He admired her fortitude when she had handed each of the children an apple while she had Scott hitch up the wagon. They went to the bakery in the village and demanded meat pies, even though the shop had already closed for the day. He was just relieved, for their sake, that the bakery still had something left from the day. And really, the baker should have been glad to sell her what was left over. He wouldn't have been able to get much for it the next day. He laughed to remember that she said the children now occasionally hoped that she burnt the meal since she didn't yet know how to make meat pies herself. Ransom figured that by now she had probably taught herself. His mouth actually watered at the thought of her cooking. He had only had one meal cooked by her, and it wasn't even that good. But he was learning from her letters what a determined little thing she was, and he was certain that she was teaching herself to be a good cook.

With a sigh, Ransom forced himself back to his feet. He couldn't just leave his claim such as it was. He needed to get at least a little bit more work done. Then he would either board it up and hope for the best through the winter or he would hire help to work it as much as possible, depending on the severity of the winter. He was leaning toward just boarding it up. Still, no one had realized that he had actually struck a vein, so he should be fine to leave it alone again. But then he would have to come out in the spring, leaving his family behind once again.

The good part about that prospect was the fact that even though whenever he read her letters or thought about Hannah he wanted to be with her, the thought of settling down and being domesticated usually gave him hives. So, if he "had" to return to Oregon in the spring, it would give him a way out, something to look forward to through the winter, if being a family man proved to be too much for his interests. While he thought she was the most beautiful woman he had ever laid eyes on and he was half in love with her from reading her letters, he had never had a desire to settle down to family life. He had only married her for Francine's sake.

As he worked, Ransom thought about what his expectations had been when he wrote to Fred and how very different the reality had turned out to be. He still remembered the thought process as he had discussed it with Scott.

"I can't take Francine with me back to Oregon. How could I work and keep an eye on a little girl?"

"You could just put her into an orphanage, couldn't you?"

Ransom's response had bordered on violent. "I am never going to allow my niece to go to an orphan home!"

"Sorry, boss, it was just an idea."

"It was a bad idea." Ransom should've told Scott why his suggestion caused such a strong reaction in him, but he just couldn't.

"What about asking one of the neighbors to take her in? I'm sure they'd be glad to do it. You could even offer to pay them a little something for their trouble."

"I don't want the girl to feel like a boarder, like she doesn't belong. I need a family for her. She's just a little girl and she's lost everything. It's bad enough the poor thing has been saddled with me as her guardian. I can't leave her to the tender mercies of strangers."

"But isn't that what you're proposing to do, anyway? If you send for a bride and then leave as soon as she arrives, you'll still be leaving the girl with a stranger."

"But it'll be a stranger she belongs to, just like me. I'm pretty much a stranger to her, too, but she knows she belongs to me. It makes a difference."

"If you say so, boss." Ransom could hear the skepticism in Scott's voice but ignored it.

"You'll see. Fred will send me some matronly widow who is thrilled at the chance to mother my poor orphaned niece. She'll be so grateful for my large house, she won't mind that I go off to Oregon. Perhaps she'll be one of those women who don't much care for men and she'll actually be delighted that I'm leaving. It'll be perfect."

Ransom laughed over the memory as he chipped away at the rock surrounding his gold, being careful not to damage the precious ore. He had not gotten what he had expected, that was for certain. The beautiful, young, elegant stranger in his house was so far from the grateful matron he had thought would step off the train. Fred hadn't mentioned her age when he had wired that a woman with two children was on her way as his wife. Fred must've had a great laugh when he thought of what his reaction would be. Ransom thought he ought to punch the man right in the face. What had he thought he was going to do with such a lovely companion? Ransom thought he had been clear that he needed to return to Oregon.

Of course, Hannah occasionally mentioned her Uncle Jason and the need for him not to know her whereabouts. However Fred knew Hannah, it would seem he was aware of her situation and the need to hide her identity. Once again, Ransom berated himself for not finding out more about his wife before he left

Nebraska. It hurt his stomach to think that she might be in danger. He tried to soothe himself with the reminder that she had Scott there and he had also taught her how to shoot. He thought with amusement about her description of her steadily increasing prowess with the gun and her disgust that Brent was quickly becoming far better at it.

I think it will have to be Brent's responsibility to provide the protection, since his aim is so much better than mine. He can shoot the knots out of your fence posts! I'm still happy if I can hit the produce sitting on the top. But of course, I can't expect that of my twelve-year-old little brother, no matter how much he thinks he's the man of the house. And besides, he'll be at school all day soon enough. So, we both are learning.

It struck him as strange that she was so determined that her brother and sister maintain as normal a childhood as possible, or at least normal from her perspective, of course, but she never wrote any complaints about how drastically her life had changed. The closest she had come was in one of her first letters.

The other debutantes would never recognize me if they ran into me on the street now, even though my clothes haven't changed. Well, they have, in fact, changed, because I've laundered them and I don't have nearly the skill that the laundress from home was known to possess. For one thing, I will admit to you freely, I despise pressing the clothes. Have you any idea why fabric wrinkles up so terribly? It isn't so bad if there's a good breeze while they're drying, I've discovered. But still, the pressing is the worst. Doing all the laundry for the four of us takes me days! Of course, that is probably because I wait until we have nothing clean left. But still. It's a dreadful chore. Anyhow, back to my unrecognizability. Even my hair has changed. I don't know why. Water is water, isn't it? I wouldn't have thought that my active thoughts would show themselves through my hair, but that is Maryanne's theory. She says I'm thinking too much and that's why my hair doesn't want to sit smoothly like it used to. I've thought of trying to press it, but I'm terrified of having the hot iron so close to my face. I'm not willing to pay that high a price for vanity. So I will tell you now, your wife has frizzy hair.

Ransom had trouble picturing her with wrinkled clothing and frizzy hair. He wondered if it was as bad as she described or if it really was her vanity speaking. He would see for himself whenever he finally returned. He wondered if she would welcome him home. She was continuing to write to him, which he took as a good sign. He wondered if she was doing it more as an outlet for her feelings or to make herself remember she had a husband. She had told him in one of her letters that it was a good outlet for her. Almost like a diary, he thought with a smile. Her letters had become more frequent. There were always at least two or three, maybe even more, whenever he went into the post office to check. It seemed as though her postage was her one extravagance. He wondered if she were writing to anyone else besides him. She had mentioned that she had written to the housekeeper. But maybe, since she was so carefully trying to avoid her uncle, she couldn't write to anyone else for fear of him finding her.

Loneliness had begun to assail Ransom. The only company he had were her letters. He admired her spirit and her fearlessness. It motivated him to work harder. It was as though she were his companion inside his head. He wondered if his letters were doing the same for her. It was like they were growing together, becoming stronger through each other's struggles.

Ransom struck harder as he shook his head from the fanciful thoughts. He had found so much gold in this vein that he wondered if the bank would even buy it all from him. They were unused to such large quantities. Besides the fact that he still didn't want word to get out about his find. He would have to take it all with him and sell it at a bank further away so they wouldn't know where he had found it. That would run the risk of it being undervalued, but he doubted it. As long as he went to a reputable bank, he should be able to get the full value. And then he would have all the money his bride might need to hire whichever staff members she might like. He would insist, if she refused.

Ransom strongly doubted any of his neighbors would care. In fact, he was almost certain at least some of them had hired help of their own. It was only reasonable. Why should the man have help on the land while the woman had to do all the work inside the house by herself? Especially when there was more than enough money to ensure she didn't have to work her fingers to the bone.

Although, from the tone of her letters, Ransom had the impression that his wife was beginning to enjoy some of her chores. Or perhaps, it was more likely that it was the sense of accomplishment those chores were giving her that she was enjoying. He didn't think she would ever come to love doing the laundry, but she seemed to enjoy when the task was finished and she could congratulate herself on a job well done. Even the time when she had scorched an iron-shaped mark onto the back of her brother's shirt. He chuckled to recall how proud she had been for her foresight.

I had figured there was a chance of my burning something so I have been pressing everything inside out just in case. Since I have no intention of buying him new shirts until he outgrows these ones, I'm relieved that it isn't ruined completely. Brent grumbled a little bit, but really, it's barely noticeable. He won't wear that shirt to school, but I don't want him wearing his school clothes out in the barn, anyway, so it hardly matters, right?

Ransom enjoyed her tendency to always look on the bright side. He marveled at her thrifty ways. He was coming to understand more clearly what a privileged background she came from, so it struck him as strange that she was so determined to save her pennies. She must associate accessing her money with the risk of her uncle finding her. And he suspected she hadn't even visited the bank to assess how much money he had left for her. Or she was intimidated at the thought of spending his money. He rejected that thought. His Hannah wasn't intimidated by anything. Maybe she was just practicing how to be thrifty in case they needed that skill in the future. Or who knows how the female brain worked? While he was enjoying getting to know her through her letters, Ransom wasn't such a big fool as to believe that he could truly know her in this way.

He would need to spend time with her in person to really know the woman.

Chapter Ten

Hannah pulled back her shoulders and raised her chin, bracing herself for meeting the children's teacher. Then she chided herself. There was no need for all this concern. She needn't explain herself. She would be contributing, just like all the other parents. In fact, one could argue the teacher was working for her. And she didn't owe him any more information than she wanted to give him.

"Good afternoon," she called out as she stepped into the schoolhouse.

"Well, hello," answered the young man standing at the front of the room.

Hannah could feel her face heating from the appreciative expression on the man's face. She quickly introduced herself and then bit her lip to stifle her amusement as his face fell slightly. "I'm Mrs. Hannah Delaney."

"It's a pleasure to meet you. I'm Bradley Smith," he answered with a polite tone. "How can I help you?"

"I wanted to speak to you about three of the students who will be coming for classes next week. One started here in the spring and the other two have just moved to town."

The man glanced down at his list of students and looked back at her with a puzzled frown. "You surely can't be the mother of any of my students."

"Yes, I am. Francine Delaney enrolled in April. And Brent and Maryanne Delaney will be starting here next week, too. Brent is twelve and Maryanne is ten. They are both quite good students, but I suppose I will leave that up to you to assess." Hannah kept her tone firm and maintained eye contact, and hoped like crazy that the color rising in her cheeks didn't reveal her discomfort.

The teacher still looked skeptical but he dutifully wrote the names down on his list.

"Besides making sure you were aware of all three children coming, I wanted to check with you to see what they need to bring with them on the first day."

Hannah tried not to fidget as the man looked at her as though she had lost her mind. That struck her as an extreme reaction. Surely, she couldn't be the only person to ask this question. Of course, he might be thinking since they were ten and twelve, surely they'd been to school before.

"We're new to town," she explained. "I just want to make sure it's the same as at their previous school." In her mind, she squirmed a little bit. It wasn't a lie. They were new to town. But she had no idea what they had needed to bring with them on their first day of school in Boston.

"Each child should have a slate and chalk, if possible. I know it might be difficult for you to provide for all three. If it's too challenging, they could share with some of the other children."

"Oh, no, we should be able to manage that," Hannah answered, trying not to hide her relief. That seemed to be a reasonable request.

"If it is within your means, they would also benefit from some paper and pencils."

Hannah nodded, thinking of the paper she had been hoarding. She would need to get hold of her wayward miserly tendencies and supply the children with some.

"Thank you, Mr. Smith. The children will be here promptly on Monday morning. It was a pleasure to meet you." She shook his hand and made good her escape.

As she walked back toward the house, Hannah laughed at her own foolishness. Her fears for the children were making her ridiculous. She determined to go to the bank the next morning to withdraw a little money. While she still had plenty from what she had brought with her, withdrawing a little would give her an idea of how much she had access to. And then she would buy a large stack of paper.

Hannah also thought about the conversation she had with her siblings the night before as she walked.

"I'll be going to meet your teacher tomorrow and make sure you're enrolled for classes," she began as the children were nibbling their after-supper cookies. Hannah had thought about sending Francine outside or to her room but didn't have the heart to cause divisions amongst them.

Brent rolled his eyes. "Do you have to, Han? Can't I stay home with you? Surely you'll need me to help you around here."

"Good try, Brent, but we've already discussed this. School isn't negotiable. You're only twelve years old. I know you're very smart, but there are still things you need to learn."

"Can't you teach me?"

Hannah laughed. "No! Can you even imagine, Brent? We'd fight like cats and dogs. Besides I'm not qualified to teach you and I don't have the time to do so."

Brent huffed an irritated breath but didn't argue any further.

Hannah bit her lip and continued. "I have to talk to you and Maryanne about something awkward and important, though."

Her tone of voice must have revealed her disquiet because all three children put down their cookies and looked at her with widening eyes. Hannah tried to smile and make light of the situation. "Don't look so worried, it isn't so very dreadful."

"You look like it's dreadful, Hannah," Maryanne whispered. "Did you receive bad news from back home?"

"Did you hear from Uncle Ransom?" Francine interjected. "Did he get hurt?"

"No, no, nothing like that." Hannah took a deep breath, hurrying to tell them so they wouldn't worry further. "It's about Uncle Jason."

"Did something happen to him?" Brent was puzzled.

"Not that I know of. Remember how you were asking me why we had to leave Boston in such a hurry and I told you I'd tell you later?"

Brent and Maryanne nodded while Francine just looked on with wide eyes.

"Well, I guess now is later. The thing is, when Mother and Father died, they left an inheritance for us. Because I'm an adult, I'm allowed to have control of my portion, but because you two are still young, yours has been put into a trust until you get older." She offered them a gentle smile, wondering if she were saying the right things, relieved that they didn't appear to be getting upset. She continued on.

"The thing is, Uncle Jason will be disappointed that he didn't inherit anything from our parents. If I hadn't gotten married, I wouldn't have been allowed to be responsible for you and Uncle Jason would have been. But I was afraid he wouldn't be nice to you and would steal your money. And I didn't want to be separated from you. So, I got married and we moved here."

Brent was staring at Hannah with a look of wisdom far beyond his years sitting awkwardly on his young face. "Are you afraid he might try to steal us away from you?"

"Yes."

"I'd rather be with you than with Uncle Jason, Han," Maryanne added, her sweet loyalty making Hannah's throat tighten. "And I don't even mind being here in Nebraska. I decided I like all the fields and space."

Hannah chuckled, recalling their conversation the first day on the train. "I'm so glad, sweetie." She hoped her *smile didn't wobble too much as she continued. "The thing is, though, I don't know if Uncle Jason is looking for us. If he is, I don't want it to be easy for him to find us. Because I got married, my last name changed. You two are still Bowmans, and we'll always be family. But I'm going to tell the teacher your name is Delaney, like me and Francine."*

Brent surprised Hannah by not being belligerent about it. "That's all right, Hannah. I guess it makes sense if you really think we need to stay away from Uncle Jason."

"I really do, at least until we're all a little older. Maybe even until you're old enough to take control of your inheritance."

Brent's eyes widened at that. "How long is that?"

This made all of them burst into laughter, releasing the nervous tension that had held them in its grip. "Years and years," Hannah answered with a giggle. "But let's just try to get through one year and see how we feel after that, all right?"

All three children nodded, making the smile on Hannah's face grow. "I just love you all so much, I can't take a chance. Thank you for understanding."

The girls got up and threw their arms around Hannah while even Brent seemed pleased by her words.

"I love you too, Hannah," Maryanne said with a sniffle.

"Me, too," Francine added.

Hannah hugged the girls tight, grateful that the uncomfortable topic had finally been broached and had even turned out to be a success.

Hannah brought herself back to the present as she neared the house. She didn't want the children to find her looking so preoccupied. Despite how well they seemed to be doing, Hannah was consciously making an effort to show them a secure, carefree existence.

~~~

Hannah frowned at her reflection. This gown had fit perfectly when they were in Boston. While it was true that she hadn't worn it in a while, she didn't think it would have stretched or shrunk with sitting in the trunk. She had been so excited when she realized that even though she had only requested the children's clothes be sent to her, the housekeeper had included some of Hannah's things, too. Especially warmer garments. They were sure to need them soon. But what had happened to make the gown be so loose?

As Hannah stood in her room gazing at herself, deep in thought, she realized, now that she gave it some thought, most of her gowns were loose. She just noticed it particularly with this one because of the heavier fabric and she hadn't worn it since living in Boston. She must have lost weight. With all the physical work she had to do, and her own cooking to eat, the combination must be resulting in a change to her figure.

Blowing a huff of frustration, Hannah threw the offending garment onto the bed. Altering it would have to be added to her list of tasks that needed to be accomplished. With how chilly the mornings and evenings were, they would all need warmer clothing very soon. Even her, although she wasn't running around outside nearly as much as the children. She was relieved that she didn't even have to escort the
~~~

children to school in the morning. It had required a great deal of effort on the first day when Brent had approached her on the subject.

"Han, I think it would be best if I escort the girls to school tomorrow. You have already met with the teacher, so you don't need to do that on the first day. It'll save you the trouble."

"Oh, it's absolutely no trouble at all, Brent. I want to be there on the first day, especially for the girls, but for you, too."

The pained look that had crossed Brent's face alerted Hannah to the direction he was going with his thoughts. He didn't want to appear as a boy.

"Surely you must realize I'm no longer a child, Hannah. I can't be needing an escort from my big sister. Or as you are allowing people to think, my mother." The disgust rolling from his voice helped Hannah keep her face straight as she discussed the matter with him.

"I understand, Brent. But do you think the girls will mind that I'm not there?"

This seemed to draw him up short for a moment and he made a slight concession. "Maybe you could walk us halfway?"

The questioning tone to his voice and the way he had tried so valiantly to sound mature at the beginning of the conversation made Hannah's heart go out to him. He wanted to be a man, even at only twelve.

"Very well, that will be a good compromise, then. I will walk with the three of you halfway, but then all the responsibility will be upon your shoulders. Are you going to be all right with that?"

The way his chest had swelled over her words let her know before he had even replied that he thought it was going to be just fine. Hannah was so proud of the young man he was already turning into. He had changed so much in the weeks since their parents had died. Hannah's heart ached over the fact that their parents, their father especially, would never get to see him grow into a man. They would have been so proud of him.

Of course, if their parents hadn't died, they wouldn't be here in Nebraska, learning and growing so much from their forced privations. Brent wouldn't be the big brother trying to be the man of the house. He would still be a belligerent little monster making his sisters' lives trialsome. Not that he had been so very dreadful before their parents died. More of a scamp than an actual burden. But after their parents died, before he pulled himself to task out here on the frontier, he had been such a belligerent little troublemaker. Hannah had wondered despairingly what she was going to do with him.

On the train, she had been thinking longingly of the husband she was expecting to take her brother in hand. Then that husband had disappeared the day after their arrival. That had certainly thrown a fly in her ointment. But she had persevered and it had all come right in the end. And now here they were. Her brother didn't want to feel like his mother was walking him to school. That was fine by her. One less task for her pile of things to do. Just as long as the girls didn't mind. But Hannah was fairly certain, with the way they idolized their big brother, that they would be just as content with his escort as with hers.

It amused her that Brent had been willing to compromise. Perhaps he, too, was a little nervous of the first day of school and didn't mind her presence so very much, but he didn't want to be shamed by it. So she would walk with them halfway, hug and kiss them all goodbye, and then stand and watch as they disappeared into their day.

A clog filled Hannah's throat at the thought. What would she do with herself for the day without the children underfoot? She thought longingly of hot chocolate and novels, how she would have spent a free day at home back in Boston. But she had already reread about six times the only novel she had brought with her. And they didn't own any hot chocolate. Both situations could be remedied, she supposed, but the mending and alterations wouldn't do themselves, so perhaps she would tackle that tedious task. It was hard to concentrate on the little stitches required when there was a constant commotion of children in the house. She would have at least six hours of straight silence the next day. It sounded decadent.

~~~

It was dreadful. She missed the children almost immediately as they had disappeared from view. She knew it was ridiculous. There had been many times when they had been off playing that they had been out of her sight for long stretches of time. But then, there had always been the possibility that they would reappear at any moment. Now, she knew, they would be all day at the school.

While it was true that she was getting many things finished without interruption, the fact was, she was
~~~

interrupting herself with constantly wondering how they were doing. She was most concerned about Maryanne, who had been undecided how she felt about going to school. Even Brent, who didn't really want to go, didn't worry her so much. He had an inborn confidence that would get him through the experience. Maryanne had seemed to take everything in stride since their parents' death, but Hannah feared the child was becoming too quiet. Hannah wished she knew how to get the little girl to open up.

Maybe she should ask to speak to the town doctor. Surely they covered matters of the heart at medical school. Hannah had to laugh at her absurd thought. She didn't really think the metaphorical heart and the physical heart were in the same place even though one's chest hurt when they were sad or upset. But she still thought the doctor might be her best source of advice. Or perhaps the town had a minister. He might know how to handle grief, since he would be expected to deal with all the funerals.

Hannah sighed as she stitched, trying to sew on a button that had mysteriously fallen off Brent's shirt. She was grateful that she had been taught mending even though it was never supposed to actually be her responsibility. But it was certainly the most useful thing she had been taught as a child. She was well aware that all the correct steps to every dance wouldn't do her much good if she couldn't lower her brother's pants hem or make her sister a new dress for school. And it wasn't at all helpful to know on which side of the plate the fork should be placed if she couldn't figure out how to provide the food to go on the plate.

At least she had been allowed to be in the kitchen as a child. She had absorbed more instruction than she had realized, a fact for which she was truly grateful. She hadn't yet become very adventurous in the kitchen but with the exception of that one dreadfully burnt meal, she had mostly had success. The children hadn't refused to eat anything she had made and while bland, most everything had turned out edible.

Hannah stared out the window, wishing her husband hadn't left. While she wasn't completely sure what she would do with him, she knew it would be useful to have another adult around. She had Scott, of course, but since he was a hired hand, she felt cautious about pouring out her problems to him. He did have sound advice when she was forced to turn to him, and he had been helpful with Brent and his belligerence when they had first arrived, but Hannah didn't feel the man had a vested interest in the success of her family like a husband would have.

A husband should be present for the moments. The moments when the children said something sweet or questionable or funny. The moments she didn't know what to say. The scary moments. The lovely moments. Hannah didn't feel adequate for all the moments they were having as a family, and she wished she had someone to carry it with her. She didn't resent the responsibilities that had been thrust upon her. She loved her siblings, and little Francine was a delight. She wouldn't back away from their care until her dying breath. But she was quite sure it would be far nicer to have another perspective. Perhaps a husband would know what to do in the situations in which she felt she was floundering. Like how to help the children with their grief.

She didn't think it was healthy that none of them were talking about it, but she didn't know how to open them up. It certainly wasn't as though she wanted to make them all cry. Heaven knows that prospect made her hold her tongue on any possible occasion. But she needed to know they were managing.

It was probably because she was too young. Hannah was afraid they realized she didn't know what she was doing. Maybe deep inside their minds they didn't trust that she could help them with their feelings.

Or maybe she was being ridiculous and they didn't even have any deeply hidden feelings. Perhaps she was projecting her own fears and grief onto them. Maybe children were just that resilient and it was really her that needed the counseling.

Hannah had to laugh. That was probably what it really was. But see, just thinking about a husband had helped her work it out. Imagine how much better it would be if she had one who was actually present instead of just one in name only. And in week-old letters. She sighed. She ought to go to the post office to see if there was another one. It would fill her empty day at the very least, she thought as she finished darning the hole Francine had managed to make in her favorite jumper. The outfit would fit the child until her next growth spurt and she loved the thing, so Hannah had to keep it functional for her.

While making sure her bread dough was rising nicely, Hannah surveyed her domain and smiled to see that everything was in its place. Who'd have thought she would take to being a housewife? And who would have thought she would miss the children? When they had first arrived out here, she had been counting the days until school started. She remembered how hard the first couple of days were and she had no idea how to keep them occupied or how to get anything done with them around. Now she couldn't seem to concentrate on much of anything for wondering how they were doing and how soon they would return.

Shaking her head, Hannah wrapped a shawl around her shoulders and stepped out. If she didn't dally too long, she could be to the post office and back in time to bake the bread so it would be fresh and warm when the children returned.

The housemaid she had finally decided to send for ought to be here any day. She needed to see if they had received any notification of her arrival. Hannah had struggled with the decision but had finally come to the conclusion that the neighbors wouldn't care. They had barely paid any attention to their arrival. Surely the arrival of one more young woman wouldn't cause much of a ripple in the small town, even if the female population were limited. And Hannah had decided she would accept the help.

She hadn't yet decided how she would pay the woman's wages, but she would cross that bridge later. Hannah was almost certain the maid would have been paid in full before she left Boston, so that left Hannah almost a month before she had to worry about it. And they had made complex enough arrangements for her travel that Hannah had a reasonable degree of certainty that Uncle Jason wouldn't be able to follow her, even if he had been having the house watched for just such an occurrence. It was still a concern though, but one she would have to try not to dwell on.

Hannah had finally figured out a way to communicate with her lawyer and her household back in Boston. One that still left her feeling reasonably protected. Just before school had started, she had taken a day and travelled by train two stops east. Hannah had explained to the children that they would be able to find their purchases more easily here since it was a bigger town than the station closest to them. She needn't have bothered. The children were just excited by the adventure of the excursion.

While they were there, she had found a lawyer's office. He had seemed pleasant and respectable and had assured Hannah that he would hold her affairs in the strictest of confidence. It had been arranged that he would receive her correspondence for her and then send it on to her real address at regular intervals. When he had laughingly told her she could have hired a secretary for a cheaper fee, Hannah dismissed his notion by reminding him: "In my experience, secretaries don't know how to keep a secret."

He had then reassured her that he would keep whatever confidences she wished to share with him.

She had already kept the children waiting so she cut the meeting short. "My address is the biggest secret I have. I expect you to guard it with your life." She ignored the confused glance he cast her and returned to the sunshine where the children were just finishing the treats she had bought them before she went in to speak with the lawyer.

Chapter Eleven

As he worked, Ransom allowed the words of a few of Hannah's recent letters to tumble around in his head. Some were light hearted and brought a smile to his face. Others were decidedly heavy.

We have finally met some of the neighbors. We stuck to the house for the first several days. Everything takes me so very long to do that I haven't had a moment to spare. Thankfully, the children have been enjoying the novelty of country life so they haven't complained that I don't have time to entertain them. But then they realized they hadn't seen anyone except each other for days and had had enough. So Scott readied the wagon for us and we went into the village.

I was surprised at the number of people we found walking the short street. I would have thought with that many people someone would have stopped by our place. But then again, I haven't gone to meet anyone either, so I probably shouldn't judge. Besides, just because people in Boston act a certain way, doesn't mean that's the only acceptable way to act, right? I do think, though, that I will try to raise Maryanne and Francine with the Eastern ways, even if that isn't the way here. There's really no harm in baking a pie and going to meet the neighbors, is there?

Ransom had found her thought processes amusing. He was glad she was finally getting settled, but he was surprised to hear the neighbors hadn't reached out to her. Maybe they hadn't realized his wife had arrived. But Ransom was fairly certain there was nothing that got past some of the older couples in the village. For the most part, everyone minded their own business, and for that he had been grateful. It was too bad, though, that the thing he had so enjoyed had turned out to be a disappointment for Hannah.

He appreciated her way of handling her disappointment. He was beginning to realize he appreciated everything he was learning about her. She was a delight. And he couldn't wait to get home to her. His feelings for her had gone way past appreciation over the past months. With each letter they exchanged his heart beat harder. Just the sight of her tidy script made his heart race. With a grin, he wondered if he would faint when he finally clapped eyes on her next.

I finally have a reason to be glad you taught me to shoot. Well, glad is too strong a word. Relieved might be more appropriate. In the last three days I have been forced to use this dubious skill twice. The first time, I actually loaded and shot the weapon. A fox was trying to get into the henhouse. Scott assures me the fright I gave it will prevent its return. I do hope he's right in his assessment. But the second experience is the sort I think you were worried about when you insisted I learn to shoot. A drunk man showed up on our porch and didn't seem to be up to any good. I didn't load the gun, but he didn't know that. It was sufficiently effective. He hasn't returned. I now understand why there are no single women in town. While I would like to think I'm capable of handling such situations, I don't really want to. Do you think your work in Oregon will be concluded soon?

When Ransom had read those words his heart had lodged itself in his throat and he had almost vomited. She was right, it was exactly the sort of situation he had feared and not wanted to leave her unprepared for. She was also right in that he should be finished in Oregon. His place needed to be there in Nebraska, protecting his family. Even if he never returned to Oregon, truly, he had enough money to last a lifetime. He had to let his poverty-stricken past go and accept that fortune had finally smiled upon him. He was rich beyond anything he had ever imagined in a monetary fashion but beyond that, he had a beautiful wife and three youngsters who needed him. The family he never knew he had always wanted. And maybe, if he were lucky enough to receive his wife's forgiveness, maybe they'd even add to the family eventually.

~~~

Ransom stepped down from the train and took a deep breath. It was surprising to him how much different the air smelled in Nebraska than in Oregon. He wondered if it was the different trees. Or maybe it was all in his head because he felt so differently about each place. But now even his feelings about Nebraska had changed, but the smell had remained the same so it couldn't be that.
~~~

He should have sent a telegram informing the family of his return. But he had decided so suddenly that he thought he might as well just turn up. Would they be happy to see him? He knew Hannah professed to want him around, but would she feel the same way in reality? Maybe she really just wanted another adult to talk to and to share the worries with.

Shaking his momentary uncertainties from his mind, Ransom strode around to the front of the station, looking for the smithy to see if he could hire a horse to ride home. He would send Scott to lead it back as quickly as possible. It was too bad he didn't know anyone who could just lend him a horse, but Ransom didn't want to waste time trying to figure it out.

The air was colder than he had thought it would be here. His fingers had been nearly freezing around the handle of his ax in Oregon before he had finally realized he needed to board things up and come home. He was satisfied with the progress he had made, though, and didn't regret the timing. He only hoped the family would be happy to see him.

Scott would be glad, he was sure. The man had actually written to him twice over the months he'd been away. Ransom smiled to think of the most recent message he had received.

Ransom,

You're being a fool to leave your family so long. Get back here and look after them before your wife fades away to a skeleton.

Scott

The man certainly didn't waste any words. He shouldn't have bothered with postage for such a short note. He could have put it into the envelope with Hannah's letters. But then again, Scott probably hadn't wanted Hannah to know he thought she was looking skeletal.

Ransom wondered for the thirtieth time what Scott had meant by that. Was Hannah not eating? Or not sleeping? Or working too hard? Or was Scott just trying to guilt him into returning? None of those options seemed likely. From what he could tell from her letters, Hannah was a sensible girl and wouldn't be so foolish as to not eat, especially not from her misguided need to save her funds. Or rather he hoped not. That thought was what had finally moved him to board up his claim and get on the train. It was still a few weeks before full winter would have set into Oregon, but Ransom hadn't been able to bear his own thoughts any longer. He would never have forgiven himself if those children were all abandoned once more because the foolish woman left in charge of them couldn't be bothered to spend her money.

Surely that couldn't be it, though. Even if she didn't spend a single penny, there were eggs, chicken, and beef right there on the farm besides the vegetables her brother was growing. No, it had to be something else. And really, whether it was just a ploy or not, it was time for him to return and take up the responsibilities he hadn't realized he had committed to when he had married that girl. Even if she wasn't the bride he had been expecting, she was the bride he got, and he ought to be doing a better job of looking out for her.

By now his wandering thoughts had accompanied him all the way home. Ransom was pleased to see that everything looked well cared for. There was a curl of smoke drifting from the chimney, which told him it would be warm and cozy inside. Or maybe she was cooking something. Either way, he'd be able to warm his hands and sit comfortably for a few minutes once he had arranged for Scott to return the horse.

He jumped off the horse and stepped through the open door of the barn only to confront the sight of his wife with her head bowed over the gate of one of the stalls and his foreman with his hand on her shoulder.

"What's going on here?" Ransom asked, hearing the suspicion ringing in his voice.

Hannah gasped, her tear-stained face rising quickly. Scott's hand fell away from her shoulder as she turned and threw herself at Ransom. He hadn't expected such a reaction, but Ransom did not hesitate in opening his arms wide and allowing her to nestle into his chest. She began to sob in earnest. It was not at all the situation he had been expecting to find.

Scott's expression was inscrutable. "Welcome home, boss. It's about time." His tone was grudging.

Ransom couldn't tell what the other man was thinking. He wasn't sure what he had walked into, but he did know he had his arms full of a weeping woman and he didn't know what to make of that. And to say that his arms were full was an exaggeration. Scott hadn't been lying when he said Hannah was fading away. Ransom was at a bit of a loss. But he did know that he didn't want an audience.

"I rented this horse from the smithy in town. Could you please take her back for me?"

"Sure thing, boss." Ransom could hear the sarcasm dripping from his hired hand's voice, but he didn't bother addressing it. Scott's issues could wait. Hannah's didn't seem like they could.

Hannah's tears were slowing and were almost dried up by the time Scott had saddled up another horse and had ridden away, leading the rented animal. Ransom suspected that she was now mortified and didn't want to raise her head. He could hear her quietly sniffing but she didn't seem to be actually crying anymore. He tightened his arms slightly before loosening them and then leaning away from her.

"Hello there," he said with as gentle a smile as he could muster.

Her cheeks were stained pink, confirming her embarrassment, but she returned his smile although hers was slight.

"I didn't expect to see you before there was snow piled everywhere, if then."

"What do you mean by the 'if then'?" Ransom frowned.

Hannah sighed. Ransom hadn't completely let her go so she wasn't able to step away from him, although it was obvious that was her intent.

"To be honest, I was beginning to feel like you were a figment of my imagination. That you were just someone I had made up in my mind and the letters you wrote were somehow manifestations of my mind's stresses. I have begun to think you're too good to be true. And I was wishing so hard for your return, I fear I've conjured you."

Ransom felt his eyebrows inching toward his hairline.

"I'm afraid I don't understand what you just said." He tried to speak gently. He didn't want to imply to her that he thought she was losing her mind, but how could she think he was imaginary?

Hannah's laugh was weak and a little watery, but he was relieved that she had retained her humor. "I don't really know what I mean, either, but I really enjoyed receiving your letters. And I've been wishing you would come back for a couple months already, so I was starting to feel like it would never happen. You never mentioned returning in your letters. And you certainly didn't give me any notification that it would be today."

As she spoke, her voice became firmer. By the end, she sounded almost cross with him. It was a relief to Ransom that she seemed to have regained her well-being, but he still wanted to know what had been taking place between her and his foreman when he had arrived.

"So, do you care to tell me why you were so upset when I first got here? And why Scott had his hand on you?"

Hannah laughed again, finally stepping back completely from him, wiping away the last remnants of her tears as she did so. Ransom allowed her to leave his arms but he felt bereft as she did so.

"Poor Scott. He must have been so thrilled to see you step through that door. He has even less idea what to do with tears than you do, it would seem. Even if the girls cry, he makes them hold it in until I get there. Which is pretty funny considering the only time they do cry is if they've hurt themselves, so it should be pretty easy to deal with. They're lovely and uncomplicated, unlike me."

Ransom was no closer to finding out what was going on but he was happy to hear from her tone that he didn't think she had any exceptionally warm feelings toward his hired hand.

"I think you're lovely even if you are more complicated than a ten-year-old."

Hannah blushed and laughed again. "Well that's sweet of you, even if it's a complete lie." She put her hand to her tousled hair and tried to brush the stray locks back from her face. "I can just imagine what a disaster I must look. In my moments of imagining your homecoming, I am always dressed in my finest, without a single thing out of place on my person or in the house. I must say, it is very bad of you to surprise us like this."

Ransom wasn't sure if she were deliberately changing the subject or if it were merely her subconscious refusing to admit to the weakness of tears. He wondered if he ought to let it go or pry into her reasons.

"Isn't this better, though? Now you don't have to fret about anything for days in advance."

"But I wanted it all to be perfect for you."

Ransom's stomach clenched. Her tone indicated there was something more afoot underneath her words. Even though he had isolated himself, or maybe because of it, he found he was able to read people's body language fairly accurately. It was apparent there was more she wasn't telling him.

"Why was perfection so very important to you?" He kept his voice low and calm, hoping she would confide in him. It might have been a foolish wish considering they had only seen each other for one day months ago, but he felt as though he knew her from her letters, and he rather suspected she felt the same way, too, evidenced by the fact that her first reaction to his arrival had been to throw herself into his arms.

She huffed a sigh. "I was hoping that if we could have everything perfect at home, you wouldn't leave again."

Ransom pulled her into his arms, ignoring the momentary resistance she put up. "I didn't come home to see a fancy dress or a tidy house. I came home to see my family."

"But is it?"

"Is what it?"

"Is this home?"

Again Ransom's stomach clenched. He now thought he understood what she was asking. She was looking for reassurance that he wouldn't leave again. He didn't know if he could give it.

"Of course, it's home." His answer was the truth; he just wasn't going to promise her that he wouldn't leave home.

"Are you home to stay?" Her hopeful tone made him ache to answer in the affirmative, but he chose to make a joke rather than tell her a half-truth.

"You'll soon be looking to get me out of the house."

As he had realized, she wasn't dim witted. Her gaze searched his face, and he could see her assessing him. Her expression cooled.

"You could very well be correct," she answered with a slight smile. She stepped even further back from him. "I apologize for welcoming you with a crying jag. Those weren't even tears of joy at the prodigal's return."

Ransom grinned. Even though he knew she was distancing herself from him, he couldn't help but enjoy her humor. Then the full import of her words sunk in and he sobered.

"I got distracted, but what exactly was going on when I arrived? Why were you so distraught?"

"Because I'm overworked and worn out and was abandoned by my husband. Is that not sufficient reason?"

Ransom grimaced. "It seems to me you've been overworked since you arrived and your husband abandoned you long ago. Your letters didn't carry the tone of a woman who gives in to her tears often. Or did you just hide it really well in your letters?"

Ransom was realizing that he might not have gotten to know her as well as he had thought.

"No, you're right. I try not to cry very often. It's exhausting and not overly helpful. But every once in a while it is the exact release that is needed." She paused, walking toward the door of the barn, waiting for him to follow. "The thing is, I'm still grieving for my family. My parents died and my life fell apart. Well, the life that I knew. I don't mind this new one, but it has been an exhausting adjustment. I worry about the children, but it seems that they have taken it more in stride than I have. And now, I've just received word that my uncle is searching in earnest for us."

Ransom's steps faltered. Her tone alerted him. She was trying so very hard to keep it all to herself and only reveal the minimal facts, but he knew there were underlying issues that were going to get murky. He should have come back sooner.

"I know you've mentioned periodically the need to stay away from your uncle, that getting away from him was your reason for marrying me and leaving Boston. I didn't want to question you over it in a letter, as it seemed sufficiently serious that you wouldn't want to write about it."

"You were right. I wouldn't have written about it. I don't really wish to burden you with it even in person. I'm still having trouble accepting that you're really here. Are you likely to be sticking around?"

Ransom didn't like her answer. She was trying to keep him out of her business. He couldn't really blame her, but he still didn't have to like it.

"Is he going to bring danger to you or the children?"

He watched as she swallowed convulsively and her gaze flicked around rapidly, although she tried to quell her reaction. "No." She didn't go into detail but they had reached the house and he had seen her gaze shift to the gun that was still propped against the doorframe.

"Are you saying no because you've learned how to load and shoot so quickly?"

Her gaze flew to his and she let out a nervous laugh.

"Could I get you a cup of tea? Have you eaten? The children should be getting home any minute."

"Hannah, don't try to change the subject. I think we should talk about this."

"Really, Ransom? Shouldn't we rather start with welcome home? How was your travel? Why didn't you tell me you would leave me so quickly? And why didn't you tell me you were returning? Do you really expect me to bare myself all the way down to my very soul without you adding a few details? I feel a little like you've become my imaginary best friend. I should have told you all about it in a letter. But now that you're here in the flesh I really don't feel like confiding in you that I'm prepared to shoot my uncle if he sets foot on our land."

Ransom blinked. She had a valid point. He had given her his heart; he just hadn't told her, and had only now realized it himself. He felt as though she had slapped him, but that was a foolish reaction. He was the one who had left her. She had a right to her reactions.

"Very well. Could you please at least tell me this before I allow you to retain your own council?"

She eyed him warily.

"From the extent of the information you have, is it likely that this threat could pose a danger in the next few days?"

Ransom watched as her eyes warmed incrementally, as though she appreciated his question. He studied her while she contemplated it.

"The children are registered as Delaneys at the school, and no one knows my maiden name. Unless he got his hands on the marriage license, which my lawyers had assured me he wouldn't be able to do, it should take him quite some time to track us. But he has his ways, so I wouldn't put it past him. Still, though, none of our names, either old or new, were on our train tickets and I posed as a matron rather than the children's older sister. Even if he has the right names, it should take him several more days to track us. On the other hand, did you get my letter about the drunk on the porch?"

At his nod, she sighed and explained. "When you arrived I was crying because I blame myself. I fear I have brought danger to the children because I couldn't handle the responsibility."

"What are you talking about?"

"I sent home for one of the maids to come help us. While I went to some effort to ensure the communication couldn't be traced to us here and had her go to a different town first before coming here, she wouldn't have been that terribly difficult to follow, I'm sure. She's an inexperienced young maid. I couldn't ask her to practice very much subterfuge. And I'm fairly certain that drunkard who maybe wasn't a drunkard was actually here to ascertain if I am who I am before my uncle comes himself. Even if he wasn't, I've received word from a lawyer I retained to facilitate communication with my contacts in Boston, that he has been questioned by my uncle via telegram. It's only a matter of time before he arrives in the flesh."

"How bad is it if it really is true that your uncle has found you? Are you in danger? Are the children?"

"Not necessarily. He has never actually hurt anyone that I know of for certain. But he has made me extremely uncomfortable since I turned fifteen. And none of the female servants care for him. It is possible that he's just a harmlessly lecherous man. But he has always coveted my father's money."

"Were you left with a grand inheritance?" Ransom was surprised.

Hannah lowered her head. Ransom wasn't the only one who had kept secrets.

"Maryanne and I were well provided for, but it's Brent I'm most concerned about. He is to inherit the bulk of our father's estate. My father's Will stipulated that his guardian was to control his inheritance until he reaches the age of majority. But it also stipulated that it could only be me if I was married. So I got married. But I'm afraid my uncle will challenge it in an effort to gain access to Brent's inheritance.

"What "it" will he challenge?"

"Our marriage," she answered, her voice tight and scared. "And the Will, I suppose, too."

Ransom watched her steadily, waiting for her to continue.

"I don't really know much of anything in detail, as you can see but, no, I don't think any danger is immediate."

"Fine. Then thank you for the welcome. I would love a cup of tea."

Chapter Twelve

annah's heart constricted and her hands felt fluttery as she bustled around the kitchen making tea for her husband. Her husband! He had returned. She had been wishing for it for weeks, months even. Really, from the day he left she had been shocked to be left alone but she hadn't been longing for him, specifically, until later. As they had written their letters back and forth, she had developed increasingly warmer feelings for him. She tried to caution herself. He wasn't necessarily the man she had envisioned from his letters. She mustn't give him her heart. She needed to preserve her heart and think about the children.

She plated a few cookies as she filled the teapot with boiling water, grateful for the mundane tasks to get her thoughts back together. She glanced up at him and then away. He looked so good. She was relieved that he had shaved. He looked civilized and normal. But so very handsome. She had seen some of the men passing through town who had been off hunting or searching for riches. They had been rough and unkempt. The fact that Ransom had taken the time to clean himself up told her he had a level of respect for her that she appreciated.

Hoping her hands didn't betray her nerves by spilling their contents, Hannah brought the tea and cups to the table along with all the other accompaniments.

"I should be helping you, shouldn't I?" Ransom was about to get to his feet.

"No, no, you've just arrived. I've got this."

"I'm so very tired, my mind isn't working quickly enough," he excused.

"It's fine, I promise." Hannah was happy to have another adult there despite her nerves in his presence.

"The children are well?"

Hannah smiled over his attempt to make conversation despite the obvious desire to question her shining in his eyes. She followed his lead.

"Yes, they are well. They have all adjusted to school. Maryanne was the one I was most concerned about as she had the most ambivalent feelings toward the obligation. But even she has decided school isn't so bad. She loves to learn. Brent, on the other hand, loves to make mischief with the other boys. And Francine just loves being with the two of them and the other students. She's so easy going. She hasn't been the least bit of trouble at all."

"Then why are you suddenly biting your lip as though there is something to be concerned about?"

Hannah laughed. "How do you know me so well even though we've barely met?"

Ransom quirked his eyebrow at her and Hannah felt heat flood her face. She realized he felt the same way as she did. Their letter writing had made them known to each other.

"I still haven't been able to get the children to speak about their grief. I haven't been able to fully overcome my own in order to discuss it with them. But they seem to be doing so well. Shouldn't little Francine be longing for her mother? Shouldn't Brent be angry that his father was taken away from him?"

"They've had you," he pointed out gently.

"But I'm not enough," she wailed softly, tears filling her eyes. Her heart and stomach clenched as he grasped her hand.

"You are enough. Even if you didn't know what you were doing, your love for them obviously shined through and reached them. Children are more resilient than adults. That's probably why your grief has been choking you while they've seemed to carry on their merry way."

She chewed on her lip some more before he reached up and soothed her teeth away with his thumb. Heat flooded her, filling her with a nameless longing. She shoved the unwelcome sensation away. Now wasn't the time.

"The thing is, with your adult understanding and concerns, you have been choked with your worries for the children as well as your sadness for your loss. You've been mourning for your parents as well as the life that you knew. The children haven't had nearly as much to concern themselves with. They have been distracted by all the newness of their lives here. But they've also been secure, knowing that you were taking care of everything. It is you that hasn't had that sense of security, which is probably why you have been struggling with your grief. Your parents likely represented security in your life before their death. You were unused to being responsible for everything. So your feelings are completely understandable."

Hannah laughed, and even she could hear the relief behind the joyous sound.

"How did you get so smart?" she asked.

"I've had the luxury of all the time in the world to think while I worked very hard at an extremely mundane task."

"So what HAVE you been doing, and why couldn't you tell me about it?"

Ransom chuckled. "I didn't tell you before I left because we had just met, and I didn't know or trust you."

"Even though you married me?" she asked drily. He offered her a sheepish grin in return.

"I trusted you with my niece and everything else that I own, but not my claim. It's ridiculous, isn't it?"

Hannah wrinkled her nose. "Claim? You mentioned that before. You mean like for minerals or something?"

"Yes, exactly, for minerals or something. Gold to be exact."

"You've been panning for gold?"

"You don't need a claim to pan for gold, anyone can do that. No, I have a chunk of land in the beautiful heart of Oregon that has a lovely, wide vein of gold drifting through its hills."

Hannah felt her eyes widen with surprise. She wasn't sure what surprised her more – the news of his gold or the clear pride ringing in his voice. She had to smile.

"Why are you so proud of yourself over it?"

Ransom grinned. "Because I accomplished it completely on my own. I found the right piece of land. I found the right rock. I dug it out with my own two hands and a pick. And I've protected it from anyone else finding out."

"Why don't you want anyone to know?"

"Because we're now in Nebraska. I'm not there to protect it."

Hannah knew her mouth was opening to form a silent, "Oh," but wasn't able to prevent it or the rapid blinking, so big was her surprise.

"So what you're telling me is that you're risking everything by coming home."

Ransom's eyes lit up as though he were delighted with her perception. "Well, not everything. I brought quite a bit of gold along with me," he replied with a pleased grin. "And I boarded everything up so no one could just stray into my mine. Of course, the boards give away that there's something to hide. But it's quite a secluded spot. And winter will close in shortly. It'll be fine."

"What would happen if someone else starts mining there while you're away?"

"Well, they'd be stealing from me."

"Could they take over your claim?"

"Only until I showed up."

"But legally, they couldn't somehow take over your claim?"

"No, I have a deed to the land."

"And if someone were to steal your gold, will you be destitute?"

"No, there's more than enough money in the bank at this point. Besides, we have this place."

He was beginning to frown, obviously not understanding where she was going with her questions. She told him.

"So, you didn't really risk all that much by coming home, did you?"

"Well, I risked someone finding out about my strike and going in and helping themselves to it."

"Sure, but you would be fine if that happened, though, right?"

Finally he returned her smile. "I'd be more than fine. Because I'm home."

Hannah sighed with relief. He was home. And that was exactly where she needed him to be. She didn't know if she could trust that he would stay put, but it was a relief to have him there for as long as he would stay. She was about to question him further when the opening door interrupted them.

~~~

"Uncle Ransom?" The joyful cry from the doorway came as a shock to the two adults in the room. The time had flown by and Hannah hadn't realized it was time for the children to get home. Before they could respond, Francine had run across the room and thrown her arms around him. It was a far more exuberant welcome than he had ever received from his young niece. He knew it was a result of her association with his wife. One more reason for him to be grateful for his marriage.
~~~

Ransom felt a little awkward hugging the small girl, but she seemed content to lean against him so he didn't want to disappoint her. He could feel his grin thinning out as he saw the other two youngsters hanging back shyly by the door, exchanging uncomfortable glances between themselves and their older sister.

"Hello there." His greeting felt a little lame but he realized, as the adult, it was his place to try to make them feel comfortable. It must have been the right thing to do because they both seemed to relax a little bit and stepped into the room.

After one more glance at Hannah, Brent stepped forward, clearly making an effort to be a man, with his hand outstretched. "Hello, Mr. Delaney."

Ransom grinned as he shook the boy's hand. "You don't need to be quite so formal with me, Brent. I'd be happy if you called me Ransom."

The boy looked bashful but bobbed his head in a nod.

It was an awkward scene and Ransom once again berated himself for having left the family so abruptly after they had arrived. While this was his house, it wouldn't have felt that way to them since they hadn't really seen him there. He looked at Hannah feeling more than a little helpless.

She must have been able to tell because despite the fact that he was fairly certain she was still feeling irritated with him, her eyes filled with sympathy and she stepped forward to take control of the awkwardness.

"Welcome home, Maryanne, Brent, and Francine. How was school?"

Francine answered right away from under Ransom's arm but he had to stifle a chuckle over the incredulous expressions on the faces of the other two.

"It was the best, and it's even better now," Francine said, making Ransom's arm tighten around her.

Ransom met his wife's gaze and grinned over the wry expression on her face. She wasn't considering it the best day ever apparently.

"I baked some cookies today." She said, changing the subject. "Would the three of you like to take a few outside so that Ransom and I can talk?"

"But he just got here," Francine protested before turning in his arms. "You aren't going to go away again tomorrow, are you?"

Guilt flooded him once more. "No, sweetpea, I will be here long enough for you to get good and tired of me, I promise."

"I'll never get tired of you, Uncle Ransom," the child vowed. Ransom's heart squeezed. A child's love was the purest gift. He had been a fool to risk it all.

"Since I just got here, Hannah and I have a few things we need to discuss before we all sit down to our supper. But I promise I'll still be here when you come back in."

Ransom was uncomfortable with the wide, serious eyes on Hannah's little sister and surprised by how readily she and her brother both accepted Hannah's edict that they go outside while the adults talked. Francine wasn't so easy to convince.

"Do we have to stay out until the dinner bell, Hannah?"

"No, not that long. Maybe half an hour or an hour. Do you think you could entertain yourselves that long?"

The little girl shifted her gaze between her uncle and his wife and then burst into a grin. "If you give us each an extra cookie."

Hannah laughed. "You drive a hard bargain, but I'll allow it this once," she answered as she added three more to the napkin she had folded the other cookies into and ushered the children back out the door.

Ransom felt nerves tighten his belly as she turned back toward him. She was such a beautiful young woman despite the weight she had lost. If anything, the air of maturity she now held around her made her even better looking than when he had last seen her. He needed her to accept him into her life. He had already given her his heart while he was on his mountain in Oregon. He only hoped she would accept it.

~~~

Hannah's stomach tightened as she turned back toward her husband. He had looked so handsome as he had tried not to be awkward with Francine. Hannah had fallen a little bit more in love with him as she watched him greet the children despite how uncomfortable he appeared to be. But a part of her wanted to hold on to her anger.

"Do you know how hard I've had to work for the last three months? I know this is your house, but I am having a hard time accepting that you think you can just waltz in and out of it without a "by your leave." You
~~~

left the day after we arrived. You left me to deal with three orphaned children. And a large house. And chickens. Do you know I had never seen a chicken in real life with its feathers still on? I had to learn how to collect their eggs so that I could teach the children how to do it. My city-born-and-raised little brother and sister have had to learn how to do chores from me, and I don't even know how to do it. And finally when I couldn't take it anymore, I sent for a maid. And now, when I could finally start to feel comfortable, now, now you show up?"

"I know, Hannah, you have every reason to be angry. I could even understand if you hate me. But I'm really hoping you'll try to find it in your heart to forgive me. Or at least give me a chance."

Hannah's heart fluttered over his words but she didn't want to roll over too easily. She kept a bite in her tone as she answered. "Well of course, I'll give you a chance. You're my husband and this is your house."

"For the last time, Hannah, it's our house," Ransom answered, frustration clear in his tone.

She couldn't help it. Hannah laughed. "You're right. Actually, at this point you might even be able to say it's my house. I've placed my mark of inexperience on nearly every corner of it. I'm most pleased to see that the floors don't show any damage from my first attempts at laundry. You did a wonderful job of building this place, Ransom. Even I couldn't destroy it."

Ransom stepped toward her, catching one of her wildly gesturing hands. It was engulfed by his large one. It made her feel dainty. And safe. She felt the prickle of tears at the back of her eyes and blinked quickly to dispel the sensation. She wasn't sure if it was anger, comfort, attraction, or joy causing the tumult inside. Probably all of those and then some.

"Are you planning to stay for a while?" she asked, hating the smallness of her voice.

His hand tightened on hers. "Like I said before. I'm home now. I never felt at home here before. I never felt at home anywhere. Or maybe I considered wherever I was to be home. But the longer I stayed away from the four of you, the more I felt that here with you was where I needed to be. I swear to you, I'll never leave you again. Not like that. I can't guarantee I won't have to go back to Oregon in the spring, but I promise I'll either take you with me or stay there only a few days if you can't come."

Hannah's eyes misted despite her efforts. It was exactly what she wanted him to say. But he didn't seem to be finished.

"I know I can't expect you to accept me fully yet. You'll probably need to get to know me a little bit more. I'm not nearly as good a letter writer as you are," he excused, seeming bashful.

"What do you mean? I so appreciated getting your letters. There were times that I thought I was wearing a rut in the road between here and the post office."

Ransom grinned. "Me, too. I kept warring with myself that I could get more work done if I stayed on my claim instead of always running to fetch your letters."

Hannah felt heat flood her cheeks. "Did I send too many?"

"No, of course not, I would have loved to receive even more," he assured her. "I've never been lonely before I left my wife behind after only one day's acquaintance. I lived for your letters. I read them over and over until they were nearly falling apart. It felt as though you were there with me in that rough cabin telling me of your trials and triumphs. It made me feel like I know you."

His voice had dropped lower as he spoke and his face became increasingly serious as he gazed straight into her eyes. Hannah's heart felt as though it were going to beat right out of her chest. She blinked furiously so her tears wouldn't hide him from her view. She couldn't speak in that moment. He continued.

"Those letters made me love you. Hannah, I know it might all be too sudden for you, but do you think you could find it in yourself to give me a chance?"

With a whoop of joy, Hannah pulled her hand out of his grasp and threw herself into his arms.

"You're so much better in my arms when you aren't soaking my shirtfront," he teased. "I know you're afraid of what your uncle might do, but you're married now. You have me. I'm not going to leave you to fend for yourself ever again. Let's make this a real marriage, Hannah. I'll keep you and the children safe for as long as there's breath in my body."

Hannah's grin felt wobbly but she offered it to him anyway. "I love you, too, Ransom. I fell in love with your words but I'd ever so much rather have you in person."

Ransom returned her smile as he lowered his head to seal her lips with his.

Hannah's smile was stolen from her along with her breath as he angled her head more comfortably. She had thought it was too soon, that she shouldn't give him her heart, but she realized that it was actually far too late. He had come home in the nick of time and everything was going to be perfectly all right.

The End

~ ~ ~ ~ ~ ~ ~

If you enjoyed *A Wife for Ransom*, you'll also like:

A Wife for Alastair

Secrets divide them. Could love build a bridge to help them overcome their deceptions?

Get it today at any bookstore

About the Author

I've been writing pretty much since I learned to read when I was five years old. Of course, those early efforts were basically only something a mother could love ☺ I put writing aside after I left school and stuck with reading. I am an avid reader. I love words. I will read anything, even the cereal box, signs, posters, etc. But my true love is novels.

Almost ten years ago my husband dared me to write a book instead of always reading them. I didn't think I'd be able to do it, but to my surprise I love writing. Those early efforts eventually became my first published book – Tempting the Earl (published by Avalon Books in 2010). There were some ups and downs in my publishing efforts. My first publisher was sold and I became an "orphan" author, back to the drawing board of trying to find a publishing house. It has been a thrilling adventure as I learned to navigate the world of publishing.

I believe firmly that everyone deserves a happily ever after. I want my readers to be able to escape from the everyday for a little while and feel upbeat and refreshed when they get to the end of my books.

When not reading or writing, I can be found traipsing around my neighborhood admiring the dogs and greenery or travelling the world with my favorite companion.

Stay in touch:

Website & Blog Twitter Facebook Instagram